HARROW THE BOYS

Published by Maverick House,
Unit 33, Stadium Business Park,
Ballycoolin,
Dublin 11,
Ireland.
D11HY40

www.maverickhouse.com
info@maverickhouse.com
@maverick_house

ISBN: 978-1-908518-66-8 (Paperback)
ISBN: 978-1-908518-65-1 (ePub)

A CIP catalogue record for this book is available from the British Library.

The paper used in this book comes from wood pulp of managed forests. For every tree
felled, at least one tree is planted, thereby renewing natural resources.

For *Lindsey, Noah,*
Willow and *Seth*

To Rick
I hope you
enjoy!

'He led us on 'gainst the coming soldiers,
The cowardly yeomen we put to flight,
It was at the Harrow the boys of Wexford Showed
Bookies' regiment how men could fight'

Boolavogue

Chapter 1

Cool saline sobs from the ring of titanium alloy that is set within the soft beneath Ram's collarbone. He puts down the wash bottle and then swabs the inside of the ring with a ply of gauze, stuffs a knuckles worth right into the hole and twists until it squeaks. Cleaning the implant makes his stump itch below the skin, all the way down to the dry socket.

Through the open window, he can hear schoolgirls negotiating the steps of the alley, a steep cleft running parallel to Market Street. He sits at his mother's kitchen table, a sturdy slab of scratched pale oak, cigarette flat and smouldering between his lips. The net curtains are yellowed at the frays and through them the Galtee Mountains wear a frozen avalanche of ambient cloud.

The arm is amputated at the elbow. Lost in the womb, strangled by fibres floating loose from the walls of the amniotic sac - it happens, pure exquisite chance. It simply turned black and floated away.

His mother, he's been told, buried it in a matchbox.

Mother is sizzling something on the stove behind him. He picks up his prosthetic from the table and slides the holster over his head. The weave is cool, the straps are rough and pinch the skin of his bicep when he closes them. Carefully he aligns the shoulder-piece above the ring, snapping it into the clasp. His stump slides neatly into the forearm cup, gentle pressure from the suction lips.

Ram's mother dumps the contents of her pan into two bread rolls, already half-wrapped in silver foil. She wraps them expertly and puts them in a white plastic bag.

Ram holds the pen-sized proprioceptor as if it's a cigar, the word *'NuHaptic'* is engraved on the metal. He thumbs a pair of nodules on the base and waits expectantly for the pairing beep. As he slides it into the hole in his shoulder, a male voice addresses him from unseen speakers: *Connecting to muscle spindle. Intrafusal fibre sync complete.*

His mother walks into his peripheral, drags out a chair from the table and sits down. She begins to roll herself a cigarette, watching the edges of her son's jaw grow tense and angular. As she watches him, what she feels isn't agony but the memory of it. It's an injury she has lived with for many years, a half-healed fracture.

Ram's index finger twitches, and to its rhythm he inhales deeply. His mother's lighter sparks. He makes carbon-fibre fists, watching the rubber knuckles stretch at the peaks and grow white from the titanium beneath.

His mother contributes to the fume, picking tobacco lint from the tip of her tongue.

'Are you bringing your rifle?' she asks.

Ram removes the cigarette from his lips, crushing it into an ashtray.

'Lazy's bringing his. Already carrying too much.'

'Bring your Dad's pistol.'

'He won't mind?' Ram replies, standing up into the smoke, wetsuit lagging at his lap.

'Just take it.'

He leans into her, kissing her cheek and the scalloped and freckled skin of her forehead.

'I will. Back in a few days.'

Ram's parents' room retains the scent from his mother's morning rituals, the sandy carpet still dusted in talc, stamped with impressions of old furniture. He takes the pistol from his father's bedside locker, apart from an old dog collar, it's the only thing in there. Whatever ammo it contains is all there is. He stuffs the pistol into a wool sock and turfs it into his bag.

In the downstairs hallway he pulls up his sleeveless wetsuit and begins dressing himself: tight waxy waders and a woollen turtle-neck, diving boots, leather apparel straps which he clasps across his chest, a re-breather and goggles, and finally his flat cap.

Outside, compressed by the alley, the drizzle is seeking him, he turns and looks out towards Aherlow, down into the drowned glen with its walnut-coloured waters, sectioned and bracketed by walls of oak and the wild antlers of Scots pine.

A month earlier he had sat in this same spot and stared down into the ocean of mist curdling around the mountains while lighting a cigarette just as he was doing now, all strung up from the letter he had fed to the kitchen grill, drowsy with the thoughts of facing another year without work. No sea-wall job, no steady income, just another year scalping copper vein and rusted engine parts from the Leak.

Then, within a week, the BRB had announced the microwave link: *Engineers with topological knowledge of the area required.* His uncle's company had won a tender with the subcontractor, and now Ram, Lazy and Breen were as good as set until August. But that was next week, this week, they were wading.

He tosses the half-finished cigarette down the alley, retrieves his sack from the ground and heads up the steps.

Chapter 2

Selwyn Heffernan is scribbling notes in his ledger, reading glasses dangling aimlessly around his neck. His shop is a re-imagined market stall frame welded to the body of an old chipper van which he now uses as office space. Inside, among wax aprons and welding masks is a dust-dappled kettle, a beige gas heater and a chipboard desk half kinked from the weight of junked drones and papers. He hears his cousin before he sees him.

'Morning, belly boxer,' Ram says through plastic bag static.

Selwyn turns around, a faintly serious look in his eyes. 'I'm fucking starving,' he says, taking the roll from Ram and sniffing it through the foil.

He unravels the wrapper and begins inhaling it one-handedly as he rummages beneath his desk on one knee. The top of his head is a salt-and-peppered grease of thinning hair. Stretched over his shirt is one of the three jumpers Selwyn is known for wearing, a tobacco-coloured thing badged with tiny holes around the shoulders and one large one in the armpit.

'No pudding?' Selwyn asks.

'We don't allow that shit in the house.'

Selwyn has emerged and is resting the drone on his lap, onions and mushroom flesh loosening from his chin.

'Now, you know this thing is lethal, don't you?'

'I know it she was just fine when I handed her to you. What's up now?'

Selwyn begins opening panels, lifting flaps Ram has never seen before.

'You've a uni-altitude drone here with a commercial fuel line tucked under a lithium polymer battery,' he says, running his fingers up and down the sting ray shaped drone. 'If a crash causes a spark, you'll find pieces of her in Bansha. Why on-'

'It's an affordable alternative,' Ram interrupts, 'Look, I just needed the camera and we're done. I barely use the petrol anyway and sure come September, I'll be rid of her altogether. And believe me, at the minute, I can't afford to be crashing her.'

Selwyn takes a conceding mouthful, flips a handhold up from the spine of the drone and hands it to Ram with a shrug. 'And will you be paying by tender or barter bond today, sir?'

Already at the bottom of the stacked cinder-block steps, Ram shouts back, 'E.C.Us, crankshafts, spark plugs - whatever I can find.'

'Now test those E.C.U's this time, will you? I don't want to be gettin' excited for nothing again.'

Ram throws two carbon-fibre fingers back at him as he exits into the heaving wind. He descends, squinting, the drone attached to his forearm.

Chapter 3

Fionntain's is the last inhabited building before Old Road, a greasy spoon with a beautiful view of the glen and a cigarette machine behind the counter. Ram knocks on the window, waving in at the Vivaldi brothers, still hunched over their breakfasts. Waiting for them to settle up, he hunkers down and fiddles with the new camera. He slips the visor on and holds the power until the display comes up. The image inside maps to the tracks of his eyes, fading in out of focus until it composes itself.

He flicks through the various views, zooming in and out and around. Lazy wanders out through the sound of the café bell ringing against the door frame. The camera whirs around to see him, iris sharpening. Ram gives him a thumbs-up, while Lazy picks his teeth with a piece he's torn off a box of matches. The elder brother is tall and formidably structured, his hair a tight number-two blade all over with a thick, patchy beard framing his perennially tanned features.

'Well?' Lazy asks. His accent is mid-western and thicker than Ram's, his Italian heritage discernible only in the cramped delivery of certain phrases. 'Any good?'

Ram unhinges the visor into two pieces at the bridge of his nose and clips both halves behind his ears. 'What can I say? The man does good work.'

Breen appears, sipping tea from a paper cup, his longer shiny hair restrained in a white hairband. Ram pulls up his sleeve, turns a switch in the wrist of his prosthetic and watches the drone lift off the ground. It performs a series of hidden but audible changes before widening to twice its size, becoming a more spindly, skeletal-framed object. He whistles through his teeth and the drone responds, returning to its default size.

'Wind's a bit strong to send her up here. We'll wait till we're on Coach Road,' says Ram, the drone landing and snapping onto his arm like a pet.

Lazy puts on a pair of cycling sunglasses and rattles his keys in his pocket. 'Will we make a move?'

'Have we a route?' Breen asks, pouring what's left of his tea into the mud.

Ram points out west.

'That way. We'll stop by Nursery for petrol, then straight on past Rossadrehid, out by the Kyle and Well. Holo Point is showing a few houses between the Wells and Garrynoe, barely touched barns, stable house, loads of stuff. Good rinse out there too, usually. We'll play there till dark, camp on the high ground and head west in the morning. Sound good?'

Breen gives an approving nod. 'Good rinse down Garrynoe, that's where the father got that picture of the basking shark.'

'Don't call your Ma names.'

Ram swats away the stealthy foot swooping for his arse cheeks, parrying with a retaliatory kick-flick to the ankles.

They trot down the hill, passing by the Christ statue and the barricade walls, stopping by the sandbag gates to roll cigarettes and adjust backpacks. The brothers begin to argue about inventory left behind. Ram watches, benumbed, as it escalates. Breen outshouts his older brother who concedes as he always does, blinking at him quietly, rifle in hand, still in its blue sheath.

When they were children, a man with wet hands guided them both into the woods and told them to make themselves into balls on the ground. When Breen started to cry, Lazy ran. If he hadn't, then who knows? The man didn't chase him, he stayed with Breen and did what he did.

It was hours before searchers found little Breen wandering alone, calling for his brother. Since then, when it came to Lazy, Breen never lost.

Inside the lot the ground is muddied beneath several species of vehicle: modified tractor trailers, a combine harvester, several variations of truck-boats, string boats and jet skis. First in line is Lazy's bruised red truck-boat, the *Lion of St. Mark*. Lazy lifts the handbrake with both hands and remains in the driver's seat while the others push from the front. The engine chokes. Again, then a series of grunts and growly hiccups that end with the vehicle starting. Lazy revs it to high heaven while the others hop on. There's room in the back for their bags and the two men, but not much else. Whatever scrap they find will have to be stored in the hull below the front of the boat, which itself isn't very roomy.

They reach a second gate of sandbags where a skinny cat lies splayed on its back, watching them with anxious eyes. A slip of a man sits in a filthy golf cart holding a paperback, looking up from beneath his white cap. As they pass, he picks a radio from his lap and mumbles into it. Ahead of them two more men appear from an aluminium cabin and roll a gear that lifts a stripped barrier. Lazy honks the horn.

They hit water at the foot of *Sliabh na Much,* right before the junction of the old coach road where the cinder walls of a repurposed B&B are marked with warnings.

Flood level amber - 4 to 7 metres. Caution: debris from falling trees.

The weight shifts inside the *St. Mark,* Ram feels it in his belly, that sudden transition to buoyancy. The truck engine cuts out and the boat engine purrs beneath them.

Immediately Ram readies the drone, which he has now christened Chinny, after an old pet that has recently passed away. He sends it up into the air, watching it liaise with the strong wind. Through the visor he sees the landscape of the glen from a bird's point of view, overlaid with augmented reality markers and a heads-up display. Wind speed, flood depth and landmarks clutter his view. Holo Point, the Irish made search-and-discovery application, loads its own slower overlay into the display. It marks wade sites, abandoned houses and farms where waders have 'checked in' and left notes and warnings for others to use. A handy app, but the information was crowd-sourced and sometimes unreliable.

'Picking up a carrier yet?' asks Breen, fidgeting with his phone.

'You should be able to connect now. Satellite signal isn't strong, though, so just browse, no downloading.'

'Password for the Cell?'

'Sycamore thirty.'

Ram checks on Lazy. The cockpit smells of wet boots and cigarette smoke.

'Too early for a pint when we get to Nursery?' asks Lazy, eyes forward.

Ram's heard this tone before. Lazy is pissed off, he can hear it in his breath, in that gulp of air he takes when he wants to say something but knows he shouldn't. His hand finds the base of Lazy's neck and he squeezes it, in that gentle conspiratorial way that men have with each other.

'You're driving.'

'That doesn't sound much like a no to me.'

Ram plucks the bottom string of the ukulele he's taken from its home beneath the wheel chains. 'She won't serve us this early on a Sunday.'

Lazy answers with his eyes still forward, tugging at his beard. 'She doesn't give a shit about that anymore, not since Larry…'

'Well, if it's going to help… '

Lazy finally looks at Ram. His eyes tell him that yes, it will help.

'Fine, one for the road then.'

Ram exits the cockpit to a fuzz of drizzle, pulls his all-weather hood over his flat cap and settles himself against the bulkhead. He feels the heartbeat of the engine oscillate up through him and he begins to tune the ukulele. The *St. Mark* glides through the narrowing channels, which soon begin to tighten so severely that the Scots pine which line the edges arch over the roads and rest in each other's arms like grieving widows above them. He plucks a single string chord to the waltzing metronome of the motors, while Breen watches videos of expensive sports cars and Lazy stuffs a pipe with tobacco. Lazy lights his pipe with an old-world table lighter he stores below the dash, and keeps them steady towards Nursery.

Chapter 4

They moor the *St. Mark* in the brothy lanes between Ballagh lower and The Windmills, boxed in by hedges of Hornbeam and Griselinia. The lane and short docking are packed with the string boats of mass goers and morning patrons. A few surviving conifers loom at them from the shallows as they wade across the old plant nursery and up onto the ramp.

The settlement of Nursery is a caravanserai market town, raised from its 45-acre bayou on timber pillars and pounded earth, decked around two tall tanks of corrugated steel - one repurposed as a Cash and Carry, the other a popular pub. A pole erected on the spot where a patron drowned holds an exhausted bouquet and is the closest thing there is to a sign post.

Tied to some fencing by the top of the ramp two horses stew about, the rims of their bellies black and prickled from mud. Strapped to the saddlebags of one of the horses is a tripod and some soft white discs used for trapping light, which Ram deduces to be photographic equipment.

Entering through the gate-less gap between the timber pillars, they notice a gathering of people. They cross the boardwalk, passing the few quaint dwellings set into the right corner of the settlement, entering a town square of sorts, parallel to the tanks. One of these is painted blue, the other canary yellow. When they've stationed themselves toward the back of the crowd a space opens, and they see what's there. Breen turns on his heel, his chest feels like gears locking.

'Fuck off! I'm going home.'

Ram eases himself through the crowd, 'It doesn't look real. Is it real?'

Breen is spiralling inwards, his stomach flipping with the ebb and flow of Ram's voice. 'I need to sit down,' he says, taking a knee behind the crowd. Lazy leaves him to it.

An older man with a rocky, purpled face turns back to them. 'She's real all right.'

'It's as thick as my leg. How long is it?'

'Ten foot, four inches. Found her by the generator farm in Galbally, caught up in the pipes somewhere trying to keep warm. Already dead when we pulled her out.'

'Where the fuck did that rinse up from?' asks Lazy, joining in the conversation.

'Pets from years ago, probably. Small nests of them adapt, hibernate in the winter. Never seen anything this big, though.'

Lazy looks back at his brother, still squatting. 'Hear that, Bree? They're adapting.'

'Go fuck yourself.'

Ram breaches the crowd, most of whom quickly losing interest, only standing around because it's a place to stand around. There's a two-man team discussing angles and poses, he ignores them, hunkering down to the snake's head. Its mouth propped open so that the internal workings of its jaws are on full, plum-fleshed display. He checks to see if anyone with authority is watching, then reaches in to stroke the teeth. Long as fountain pens and smooth, they're more impressive than terrifying, although the four rows of shorter backward-curving teeth which line the roof of the creature's mouth trigger a vestigial panic in Ram lost to him sometime back in the Palaeolithic. He discovers, almost peripherally that he has been holding his breath.

He spits a lance of phlegm at the ground. 'Hope you find yourself somewhere warm wherever you are, buddy.'

Lazy is still in the crowd, twiddling the beard at the edges of his jaw, thin tight twists that whip his earlobe when he lets them go. He does this when he's thinking, when he watches television, when he drives, he does it until it hurts, until he has to shave the beard off. Then he starts again. Ram gets a wink from him as he passes. Breen, still squatting, feels a tug on his hairband. Ram suggests he may need a drink. Breen gets to his feet, glancing malevolently over his shoulder at the strung-up python, it turns out he does.

The Bully Vogue is a deliberate mispronunciation, derived from the way Maureen Glynn's son pronounced the rebel tune Boolavogue when he was a child. Inside, the pub exists in its own kind of dim light. Its ceiling rafters and cylindrical walls wear a warming shell of bruised mahogany, reclaimed from drowned-out venues once famous in town-lands like Emly and Lisvernane. The same walls are decorated with displays of bronze keys and hurleys, 1916 proclamations, French and Italian flags, retro signs selling pitch stout for pennies, and bleached-out photos in plastic frames. There are sprigs of tinsel left tacked into the beams, catching candlelight since last Christmas or perhaps the one before.

Beyond the bar, with its frame of frosted rustic stones, the back wall hosts half a dozen cots for patrons too drunk to make their way home. There are still some sweaty heads snoozing in their shoes above the blankets as Ram and the brothers amble in from the damp. The fire is being lit, the bar being cleaned, the air smells of citrus and nutty brass polish. Men are already at the bar, but not many, rubbing their small heads with swollen hands, thinking loudly, some mumbling, sniffling from sleep.

Ram tells the lads to pick a table while he goes up to order. He knows what they want, doesn't even have to ask.

'Two pints and a whiskey-ginger, please,' he asks the barman, a long lad with measles marks in his cheeks. His name, to the best of Ram's knowledge, is Tim.

Tim looks up at him from the Slim Jim he's wrenching clean. 'Ye talking to the river already? Not even twelve.'

'Talking to whoever answers,' replies Ram, scanning the length of the bar down to the man at the end with a black-and-white collar round his neck, sucking on a can of cider. 'Jesus, what's the story there?'

'He's the one who got the call in for Carneycross.'

Ram's eyes squint into slits. 'What was that, now?'

'The family that got swamp-bit in the field near Carneycross? You didn't hear?'

'I didn't. A whole family? Fuck's sake, were they drinking from it? How does that happen?'

'Bio-engineer and his family, wife and daughter, set up camp near the fairy ring, they had fancy hanging tents, the whole shebang. There's three different signs and a fence there in places. Didn't see 'em. Willy Ryan's crew passed by the next morning and saw the set-up. They knew it was bad but they'd no gas masks to go in. Bad aul shit, Jack.'

'That gas is no joke, slurry under there thirty years that'd strip the skin off the soles of your feet. What was he thinking? Fuck me, did nobody cop them?'

'Sure, who's going to cop them out here? When the spacesuits went in, the daughter was the only one still had a breath in her. They called himself in to deliver the last rites. I don't think he's the better of it.'

'She dead?'

'Oh, she's dead, Jack.'

Ram took the pints to the lads and headed back to the bar, still mulling over the story in his head.

'Here, give us a can for him.'

Father Browne is slim, pale and avian-faced. His chest is flat, almost concave, filled with hollow bones. He has a top-fro of curls clipped tight at the sides. His shoulders are bunchy and dappled with dandruff.

'Father,' says Ram, dropping his gift on the bar.

Father Browne gurns out a smile and palms the stool next to him. 'Master Gallagher, you're very good. Join us for a minute, go on.'

Ram slides onto the stool, pours the ginger ale into his whiskey and takes a sip.

'Rough one, I hear.'

The priest blesses himself the lazy way, two tips on the forehead, chin and chest, 'Roughest in a while. Roughest in a long, long while, but that's the work. Tell us, how's the mother?'

'She's good now. The cataracts aren't so bad anymore. She gets them lasered in Limerick twice a year. Usually have to drag her there by the hair, but - you know, better than her going blind.'

Browne knocks back the last swig of his can and drops its carcass behind the bar. He strokes his forehead with his fingers, so badly stained at the tips that they seem almost green.

'That's good, that's good. Fine woman, your mother, fine person, I mean.'

Ram is close enough to smell the man: a powdery hum, hung with notes of ammonia. The priest mumbles something to himself, possibly in Irish. This mumbling trails off into a jerky head movement which ends in uncomfortably intense eye contact.

'Can I ask you a question, Raymond?'

'Sure you can.'

'Tell me, if you will, what do you think happens when you die? From your perspective, the Catholic view, which you would have been taught in school. I'm just curious.'

Browne cracks open the cider and tips it down his throat. Ram takes another sip of his drink, biting his glass gently while he considers his answer. He imagines the priest holding the girl above the waist-deep water as if in baptismal ceremony, whispering the last rites into her chest as her head collapses and her eyes roll back into their sheaths. It can't have been easy or nice. Browne was a decent skin when he was sober, visited Ram's mother when she needed visiting. He feels the need to give the priest these few moments of company. It was in his nature to ease the suffering of things.

'Wow, that's some question.'

'It's not a test.'

'Well, you go to Heaven, unless you were a bollocks, pardon my French.'

The can of cider is sweating cold, the priest runs a channel down through the condensation with the tip of his thumb. He gurns again, smiling doesn't seem to suit his bird face. 'Heaven indeed. She thought the same, Lisa, the young lady who passed away. Terrible, Raymond, just awful. She asked me if that's where she was going. Her little lips were so dry they were black. I said, "Yes, you're going to heaven, Lisa, and your mammy and daddy are waiting for you there with Jesus Christ our lord and saviour". I blessed her with the oil and got her to say a "Hail Mary" with me. She was gone by "the fruit of thy womb, Jesus".'

Ram feels out of his depth here, it's all escalated a little too quickly, getting a little too honest for this early on a Sunday, but he goes along with it. Who was he to judge a sloppy drunk? The day-drunk get loose-lipped, that's just how it goes, God knows he'd been there enough times.

'Don't think there was much else you could have done, Father. I'm sure you gave her some relief. It's a very hard thing to do. A lot of people take that part of the job for granted, very hard thing to do.'

'And you've never heard of *Sheol,* or the one thousand years?' the priest asks, shifting suddenly in both position and tone.

'Eh... yes, the thousand years. We got all the literature from Father Laughlin back when it happened.'

Father Browne grasps his cider, yanking it back like a pilot's yoke.

'Ah, you have to know the rules, Master Gallagher. Nobody knows the bloody rules these days, there's a lot of administration to the afterlife, you know.'

The priest's eyes go the wet sort of vacant and his jawline gets lumpy, as if he's chewing down on what he's thinking, 'The devil is in the detail.'

Ram detects a creeping indignation in his voice which is probably best left alone. He takes it as an opening.

'Well, I just wanted to drop over to offer my support, Father. I should probably head on,' says Ram, presenting his hand.

The priest grabs the cold hand by the wrist and shakes it.

'Good man. God bless.' He turns his hand and Ram's with it, pulling back his sleeve to check his watch. 'You'll make 12:30 Mass now if you hurry.'

Ram turns a laugh into a cough. 'We'll see what we can do, Father. Take care.'

He walks away from the priest in a daze, flopping in beside the two lads. The weather and corrugated steel has killed the phone signal, so they're both staring glumly into their pints.

Ram skulls what's left of his drink.

'Riveting stuff, lads, don't let me interrupt. I'm going to get the petrol.'

He makes to leave when all of a sudden he feels the soft edge of a beer mat bounce off the back of his head, then another to the cheek while he's turning. Breen is leaning back in his chair, arms behind his head like a brat.

Ram sighs audibly. 'Have you two geniuses tested your re-breathers lately?'

Lazy looks up from his pint, his beard now a bifurcating nest of twiddles. He plucks the beer mat from beneath his pint and flings it, all wrist so it glides perfectly without drag or yaw. Ram snatches it impressively just as it passes between his shoulder and cheekbone.

'On the ramp in ten,' he says, firing it back.

Ram pauses in the pub's doorway, a great big yawn in the wrinkled steel, packed with timber and painted that hideous Tipperary yellow. He lights a cigarette, inhales the warm rustling textures of British-American tobacco and watches the bustle.

Business owners are wandering, dropping vinyl mats, staring at the sky, conducting meteorological assessments with wet fingers. Smoke from log fires hovers like a warm breath.

Maureen Glynn is at a coffee tent, leaning in over the counter like she owns the place and talking to a girl, a nail-biting teen with a shaved head and enormous eyes. Maureen is in stretchy jeans and a fleece, her hair in a wet twist at the back. Ram knows her to see, but not well enough to bother with a greeting.

The vague chorus of prayer can be heard from beyond the market, where the parish chapel stands, the archbishop's voice deep and echo-amplified. The sizzle of meat finds Ram and he follows it through the stalls, water globules thick on the treated wood. Boardwalks shouldn't creak like this one does. Crêpes are being folded for a man and his little boy, chocolate and banana with pinches of coconut. Juices are being squeezed, cupcakes ignored, trout selling well.

He haggles with the canister man, but it isn't Dessie this time - it's a new guy with nose hair and a grandstanding attitude, he isn't playing ball. Fifty quid later, Ram is carrying the four petrol cans back to the ramp where the brothers are waiting. Breen is petting one of the horses, feeding it chewing gum and whispering into its mane. Lazy is on his phone playing poker.

'How much did you get it for?' Lazy asks.

'Thirty five cold.'

'Same as last time. Couldn't do better?'

'I just wanted to get getting.'

Chapter 5

Luca Vivaldi was born with a lazy eye, a congenital imbalance in the ocular muscles controlling movement. He wore plastic corrective glasses from the age of two and an eye-patch three hours a day until he was seven. Doctors tried chastising it with paralysing agents, lasers, stem cell eye drops, but nothing worked. This had left him with blurred or double vision, prone to nausea, vertigo and headaches. The muscles were not corrected surgically until he was eleven years old. It required four separate interventions over two years.

Luca remembers the day the last patch came off. He recalls traveling with his mother to the children's hospital in Naas - the smell of the ward, the dark-skinned doctor with long hair that peeked out from beneath his ears, his sharp inhalation as the torch went out, his grey teeth.

Afterwards his mother had brought him around Hibernia, to the fancy markets above the Grafton arcade, where a mad woman danced alone on the street and a man sat on the pavement and sculpted a shark out of sand. She bought him a car magazine for the train ride home and a video game to share with his brother. Then they took a short bus ride to the sea wall, where they ate chunks of chips with wooden forks and climbed one of the *cloigthithe*. They sat at the top and watched the sun faint into the drowned city. In the dark, the city was an approaching armada. What a thing to see with his own two eyes.

There is some movement within his peripheral, something

slender noiselessly bobbing within the treeline. Lazy pauses in the flood, his rifle available to him. A fox is frozen elegantly on a low branch, mouth clamping a grubby pelt, dry, gory. It regards the man with dim eyes. Lazy reaches into his pocket, slowly so as not to startle, produces a comb that opens like a straight razor and strokes it through his beard. The fox looks away and then back again, then away and back again. Lazy turns first, and when he looks back all that remains is the wagging branch.

Splitting up to cover more ground before dark, the three haven't spoken in nearly an hour. Lazy is two fields deep when he notices the boat, heeled over on its side, belly exposed. It has the red-and-orange stripes of a patrolman, an old winter lifeboat. He holds his rifle with both hands above his head. This gives him a sense of infantry. Walking in the rib-high water makes him feel adept and invincible.

The gash in its hull is wide enough to walk through. Inside he finds nothing of any value, all that's left to take is the boat's dashboard compass, globe cracked and drained of its fluid, needle resting on east. The engine has been stripped, a surgical scar on the gunwale is the only evidence it was ever there at all. A length of rope wrapped around the cleats is so dank it isn't even worth taking. The hull could be worth something, provided anyone had the want to strip it down.

Lazy takes his phone from his chest pocket and marks the location as 'empty' on Holo Point. As he considers where to go next, he notices something peculiar about the treeline ahead of him, the woods are sheared, trunks ripped apart or tipping over into the water, as if something massive had burst through. He wades across, sloshing uphill. The monoxide monitor around his neck blinks green, so he removes his mask and lets it rest on his forehead.

As he climbs the banks a bed of blackberry bushes scratches at his waist, finding skin beneath his shirt, staring up at him with spider eyes. He digs the stock of his rifle into the mud to gain a handhold and drags himself up onto the forest floor. His legs ache and he feels as though the bristles have scratched him deeply enough to draw blood. He retreats inwards for a moment, remembering his father telling him that viruses kill twenty per cent of all life in the oceans, daily. Lazy recalls the time Breen caught Staph - he had to keep the shin wound open and filled with antibiotic pellets which looked for all the world like tiny blue breath mints. It was the most disgusting thing he's ever seen, candy pearls and rotting flesh.

He should have worn wets beneath his clothes, but they get so fucking hot when you're not in the water. He stands in the clearing, regarding its subtle oddness, he's staring down into a channel of sorts, an artery carved into the forest. What did this? No rinse is that strong, not this year at any rate. It's not enough to do this kind of damage and even if it were, where is the debris? It would take a bus or truck or yacht to do this, not to mention one hell of a current.

The air is sour with sap and bog water. The sky is losing light. He paces the breadth of the channel, searching for clues: tyre tracks, tank treads, pieces of meteorite. A quilt of branch tangle looks easy enough to peek under, but as he lifts it something happens beneath him, a sudden thrashing that bucks him backwards on his arse.

'*Porca troia!*' he shouts, forgetting to translate his thoughts on the way out.

He readies his rifle, shaking, half expecting a snake the size of a house to shove its head out through the thicket. There's a noise now, a sort of piggy sound but not quite high-pitched enough, a soft snoring or maybe whickering. Lazy rises to his feet, reaching out slowly to the nearest branches, he grabs the very tip of one and runs it backwards, rifle resting on his hip. There, lying in the mud, is a horse, a horribly injured horse.

He takes a breath, feeling relieved but squeamish. The horse is crippled, its hips twisted and deformed, bones breaching its copper coat, the same coat he had seen sagging from the fox's jaws.

A whisper comes out of him, *'Gesù...'*

The stench is so bad that he puts his rebreather back on. The horse's behind is a bale of gore and excrement. It still bears a saddle and bridle.

The ground beside the horse is indented with deep straight lines - a track of some kind, three clear impressions in the earth. Something heavy was here: weighty enough to crush a horse. He looks at the animal, whose head is rocking back and forth. It breathes intermittently, an awful respiration, too weak to be described as laboured. Lazy takes out his phone.

Four fields east, Ram is shoulder-deep in the brown water, his '60s bleak-rock so loud in his ears that they tickle. After ten minutes of wrestling, he finally spins the rotary shield loose and yanks it out. Chinny is hovering five feet above the water, a net suspended from the drone's belly is holding some bits and bobs Ram has scavenged - an old hand-held games console, a bicycle chain, Ram's jacket and jumper, and a half-dismantled power shaft from the skeleton of the tractor he's been stripping.

He stands up and stretches his back, his wetsuit welded to his body, his tool belt spilling water. Ram plays with the movable pieces of the rotary unit, assessing its weight and value before placing it in the net. He's going to need to burn through the chassis to get to the engine block. The flame is thick, efficient and cobalt blue. The phone rings in his ears just as he begins to line up the cut. He pulls out the headphones, swiping a small screen in his wrist.

'You all right?' he asks, clearing his throat.

'I can barely hear you.'

'The thing in my headphones is fucked. You're on speaker,' replies Ram, shouting.

'I've got to fire a shot here. Just giving you fair warning.'

'A shot? At what?'

'Found a horse. She's in ribbons, I'm putting her out of her misery. Ram, there's something fucked-up going on over here.'

'What's up?'

'Forest's been starched flat by something.'

'Probably something dragged along in the flood.'

'Well, it crushed a horse and I don't think she was out for a swim. I think something was chasing her.'

'Any sign of a rider?'

'Nope.'

'Hold on, your fuckhead of a brother is trying to call me now too.'

'Hey, don't answer yet.'

'Why not?'

'Don't call him shit behind his back.'

'Jesus, I was only joking.'

'I know, Just, please don't.'

'Fine, whatever.' Ram swipes the screen to answer the other call.

'What's up?'

'You sound weird.'

'Cool. Story? What's up?'

'I can't get through to the other cunt. Is he with you?'

'I'm here, fuckhead.'

'We're all here. What do you want? I'm stripping a tractor.'

'I have a tanker here.'

'You have a what?' asks Ram.

'A tanker without its cab. Markings are all washed off.'

Ram is already clipping his blowtorch to his belt. 'Okay, don't touch it. If it's oil or gas it could be dangerous, need to frost her first. Any smells in the air? How's your monitor?'

'Smells like shit, normal. Monitor is green.'

'You see anyone else around, Bree? Horses or anything?' asks Lazy.

'No, all quiet. Why?'

'You're standing beside twenty-four-carat gold. Stay low. We're on our way.'

Lazy hangs up. One second later, a gunshot sends a squadron of crows across the field.

'What the fuck was that?'

Ram says, 'Don't worry about it,' and hangs up.

Lazy and Ram cross the field from opposite corners, their foamy wakes trailing in converging lines. They meet an acre or two ahead of the tanker, a dull chrome cylinder nested in thick hedging between fields. Breen is sitting on top of it pretending to light a cigarette, breaking his hole laughing at a reaction they haven't yet given him.

'You're hilarious,' says Ram, placing his hands on the chrome.

He unclips a device from his belt, it has a handle and a rectangular screen. He holds the device flat against the tanker's hull and turns on the display, pinching at instructions as they pop up.

Lazy hovers at his shoulder. 'See anything?'

'Hold on. I don't know if you can X-ray through whatever this is made of.'

The screen brings up an image, black with vague unmoving impressions. He smacks the hull, watching the shivering impressions on screen. 'Okay, I can see through it but I don't know what the fuck I was thinking I'd see. It moves a bit when I hit it. Who knows, it could be oil.'

'Fuck fibre!' shouts Breen. 'We're rich!'

'Relax, Bree,' says Lazy automatically.

Ram clips the device back onto his belt and unclips another, a drill-shaped tool with a broad, round flexible nozzle defined by a wide protective collar: a foam gun. He loads it with a cartridge stored in his chest strap.

'Hey, the man could be right,' he says, placing the nozzle against the chrome. 'Let's find out.'

Pulling the trigger produces a sound like the last dregs coming out of a can of hair mousse. He moves the nozzle away and immediately cleans it with a rag from his pocket, tossing the rag into the water where it sizzles gently. There's a clump of foam left on the hull of the tanker, enough to fill the bottom of a mug, it is dry and as pale as mashed potato. Ram produces his water bottle and begins to pour water onto the foam.

'All right, lads, look out, we're using technology.'

The excitement tugs at Breen, sliding him down the hull and into the water. The hissing has a violence to it that tells them not to get too close. When it stops they crowd around it while Ram examines its new texture and sound. He uses a screwdriver to poke at the petrified foam and it chips away with the crumbliness of stiff pavlova. The screwdriver goes in all the way to the handle and stops.

Ram turns to the others. 'Here we go. If she starts bleeding, plug her. Who's got the medical putty for the edges?'

Breen tosses his medical putty to Lazy, who is already waving the boat plug in his hand. 'Try not to waste an ounce.'

Ram takes a stiff breath in through the nostrils, cocks his arm and rams the heel of his hand into the handle of the screwdriver. He feels it poke through the other side and quickly steps aside to let it spurt. Nothing happens. The three look at each other in varying states of confusion. Ram regards the head of the screwdriver, which wears a garter of some shiny liquid, thick and flaxen-coloured.

Then the smell hits them.

'Jesus Christ! What *is* that?'

'I don't know, but it's fucking malignant.'

'Can petrol go off?' There's a desperate, failing hope in Breen's voice.

The tanker moves in what seems like a seizure, rocking forward and then all of a sudden upwards. The three make quick, silent, independent decisions. Retreating, Lazy grabs Breen by the arm and yanks him back. A series of bulges pop from the tanker's skin, the hole is swelling and widening, weeping thick cultures of what looks like mould.

'Fucking run!' Ram shouts, and as they turn the tanker bends and bursts apart, sending a torrent of white, grey and green heaving outwards. Ram, being the closest, is lifted from the water and dropped back in face first. The brothers are knocked to their knees, and in a panic Lazy forces Breen's head underwater.

Disturbed birds cramp the skies, descending to the trees like air-dropped leaflet propaganda. What's left of the tanker tips itself into the water. The three rise slowly from the gunk, covered in the stinking goo. They look at each other, profiles lumpy with fist-sized clots of the fetid milk, evolving quickly into an eighty-year-old cottage cheese. The world smells like something rotten and half-digested. Lazy lets a chunk fall out of his mouth, followed by vomit. Ram and Breen are bent over laughing, ears ringing.

'Fuck off,' gawks Lazy between pukes.

Ram wipes his face with an equally messy hand and whistles. Chinny zips down from the fading sky. Ram gestures to Breen, and he moves in. All three huddle in close while the drone snaps a picture, bursting their holes laughing at the state of things.

Chapter 6

They reach the *St. Mark* before dark, trudging humourlessly up the lane where they left her. The light is the last few embers left behind the mountains. Weather was coming, and the sky sounded angry with thunder. In a flurry, the three strip by the side of the boat. Lazy leaps in, still naked, working to get the canopy tied up while the wind is snapping it. Ram dumps a two-litre bottle of antibacterial soap into the water and drops down into it. Breen holds the shower bag over him, but the water skits away before it even hits his head. The rain seems to go from a whispering drizzle to storm without any in-between.

Ram holds his prosthetic in his armpit while he fiddles with the drone's controls, if he doesn't get it down quickly he's likely never to see it again. He switches to the petrol supply and they watch as Chinny burns a tramline through the sky.

Inside the soft-top canopy two fan heaters share the same socket, the ratty extension cord propped up out of the wet by a plastic crate draped with towels. The three dry themselves, patting their skin with anti-fungal talc and holding their feet to the heater.

Lazy opens a hatch in the cockpit and takes the dinner his mother has prepared from the cooler. He unplugs the heaters so he can use the microwave, an off-white block that still has splatter marks from the previous year. He takes three plastic plates and drops fistfuls of salad on each while the microwave turns. The salad is crusty bread, cherry tomato, rocket and chopped pickle.

The microwave bings and out comes the chicken patty with pasta and beans, which they drink from mugs with the homemade bread floating gluey on top.

Ram settles back into his nook against the bulkhead. He brings a blanket up around his shoulders, pulling it in tight against the damp. There is something about the white noise of rain on the tarp, with the breeze on his feet and the soup in his hands. At home he doesn't sit still indoors, out here is where he feels rested, out in the tame wilderness of the glen. He only wishes there was a pit-fire to stoke and tend, or the bad weather to have passed so he could stare at the sky while he waited to sleep. That would be perfect.

Breen is still bellyaching about the coverage being gone, but the wind would have twisted the drone into a knot. Lazy's just happy he texted his mother earlier, it would have chewed at him all night to think she was waiting up late for the message. He hooks a lamp up to the tarp and the three start smoking weed from a porcelain pipe. They play cards while some music crackles from the boat radio.

'How's the father now?' asks Ram, dealing.

'He's a *Slán*,' Lazy says sharply. 'That's how "the father" is. He sleeps in the sitting room. You hear him opening cans in the morning, pisses into them through the night sometimes, forgets about them by the next day. Mam empties them down the back of the garden and thinks we don't see her. Anything else you want to know there, Ram?'

'Jesus Christ, take it easy! Your mam made dinner, I'm just asking.'

'You're asking because you're bored. I don't want to bitch about my dad, or tell you about him falling asleep with the deep-fat fryer plugged in, I just want to get barbecued and play poker.'

Breen toasts the air and cracks open a can, offering it to Ram.

'I'm fine. I'm taking a Xanax in a minute, I'm wrecked.'

'Don't be a baby.'

'Are we going diving in Waterford or what?' Breen asks, just because.

'Why? Why would we be doing that?' Ram massaging his forehead with the heel of his hand.

Lazy answers for him. 'He wants to dive down and steal a Viking helmet from the museum. You know, because he's an idiot.'

Ram stretches his hand out. 'Changed my mind. Give me one of those.'

The cider and weed has Ram out cold within the hour, but he wakes again through the night, sleeping bag knotted around his legs. He squints for a few moments at Breen who is still awake, drinking, head nodding to whatever he's listening to in his earphones. The wind is blowing but calmer. He gets on his knees and looks outside at the water: dark, sleek and rippled like vinyl. The air is cool and his cheeks feel hot from sleep. He turns off the light. Lazy is in the cockpit asleep with his feet on the dash. Breen doesn't say a word, just continues to nod in the dark.

Chapter 7

It is mid-morning before anyone is fresh enough to start moving. Lazy stands bare-chested on deck, sipping black tea. He never wants to taste milk again in his life. Breen has emptied his stomach, manually, but it hasn't helped. Ram is by the back of the boat scouting the area with his goggles, tapping away at the screen in his wrist. He tags four houses, one at the end of the narrow where they've moored and three more a few minutes' wade west from there. Lazy spills his tea overboard and fires up the engine.

The *St. Mark* gets five minutes up the road before Breen asks him to cut the engine so he can jump overboard and empty the only hole he hadn't yet evacuated. Ram tosses some toilet paper down to him but he's too doubled over to catch it. He wipes with soggy paper and lies on the floor of the boat while Lazy fumes about it up in the driver's seat.

The first house is relatively well-preserved, old-world stone walls, single storey. It is submerged to the ground floor windows and wears a silty scum which in places is as thick as ivy. They leave Breen in the boat, Lazy giving him a stiff jab of his boot on the way.

Inside the house is gutted, bones picked clean. The walls have been opened, deep channels dug out of the plaster in sharp-angled calligraphy, pipes and wires extracted surgically, nothing left but dry veins.

In the kitchen all the broken-up storage units are piled into a corner, leaving only the shadows of plumbing on the walls. They could check the attic, but the ceilings are buckled and dented and it's not worth the hassle. Leaving through the back door, grumbling to each other, they notice Breen pulling at something in the bushes. They help him yank the old motorbike from the thicket that's grown up through it and drain the gas tank for a good gallon and a half, which is something at least.

By mid-afternoon the sky is dark and gathering clouds. The three wade about by the walls surrounding Kyle and Well, searching the foam for holy bubbles. Ram has promised his mother that he'll bring home some water from St Berrihert's well, but the underground spring is playing hard to get. In the end the rain comes, so he just bottles whatever is floating between his legs.

'This is horseshit,' announces Lazy. His legs are cramping, so he leans down on his thighs in a half-squat.

Ram has seen this coming, there has been tension in the air since lunchtime. He's caught the brothers texting each other stealthily, exchanging hand signals and exhaust-pipe breaths. They seem closer for it.

'I know,' he says, speaking at the bottle cap he's tightening.

'A few mugs of petrol and a U-length? Sure that isn't worth a shite, man. Are you able to use that thing?'

Ram knows this pattern. Cue Breen any second now.

'Shut up, Luca, will ya?'

His knight in shining armour.

Probably called him every name under the sun ten minutes earlier.

Lazy flaps the air, 'I'm the dickhead that's going to be driving half the night, while you're micro-dosing mushrooms again. My legs are killing me and there's fuck-all to show for it.'

Even when they're on the same side, everything always collapses into one of them versus another. Their relationship has a recursive geometry to it, a mathematical quality Ram hasn't fully figured out, but he's spent enough time around them to realise when a line was going to bend or break.

'Relax,' says Ram, hands up. 'We've half a day left, so let's just check what else is around before we lose the head. This is a good spot, they're not finding trucks of milk in Galbally.'

'Jesus, aren't we fucking lucky,' jibes Lazy, grabbing the headset from behind Ram's ears. 'Let me have a look at that thing.'

'Help yourself, dickhead,' replies Ram, holding out his wrist. Lazy plays with the controls set into the wrist of Ram's arm, head wobbling, trying to figure out what he's looking at. Breen is in his peripheral vision, grabbing his balls and giving his brother the finger.

'There,' Lazy announces, 'through the woods. Stables and barn. It has a fucking fountain in its driveway.'

'East 12?' asks Ram.

'Think so, yeah.'

'I've been looking at it all day, you numpty. The app says it's been stripped and shipped. Reviewers all verified. It's bullshit.'

'Hmm ...'

'What?'

'If it's bullshit, then why is there a generator inside the barn?'

Ram yanks the headset off him. 'What are you talking about?'

'Did you use the infrared?'

Ram looks through the visor: it's an overhead view of the estate filtered through the fuzzy blue tones of infrared. 'We haven't really been close enough. I just read the tags. I don't see anything, where are you getting a generator from?'

'Back corner of the barn. Two squares with a bunch of

lines connecting them, probably high-end diesel.'

'Shit, you're right. That's not a barn, either, it's open at the front like the cover for a silage pit. If I go down lower, I bet I'll see the laths laid out.'

'Shouldn't be silage that close to a house, unless they're thick,' adds Breen.

'Someone trying to honey-dick us, Ram. There's a decent haul there. Fact.'

Ram snaps the visor open. 'Definitely some sort of fuckery going on.'

Lazy pulls up his hood, preventing the rain from crawling down the back of his neck. He claps his hands and rubs them briskly. 'Well? Are we getting involved?'

Ram and Breen look at each other and shrug indifferently.

'*Eccelente.*'

Chapter 8

After navigating the stagnant pond of a road that separated them from the estate, the three crank themselves over the chest-high gates and begin to sog their way up the driveway, a long curving lane lined on both sides with a light-dimming knit of some fancy hybrid willow. Traversing the mud is a job - the green water in the lane is shallow, but walking through the suck of mud beneath is like one of those disturbing chase-dreams where your legs keep getting stuck to the ground when you're trying to run from the murderer.

At the top of the lane the house and barn are surrounded by a two-tone wall of ornate stone extended with cavity blocks. Dull chips of black and green glass are set right on top of the concrete coping, inside a gnarly whorl of barbed wire. They approach the gate, two rusty squares chained together and padlocked. Ram gives them a rattle, kicks the sandbags at the foot of the gate and calls behind him for bolt-cutters.

Breen passes him his cold saw. 'You see bolt-cutters anywhere, dumb-arse? Use this.'

Ram appraises the blade, pulls the trigger and winces a little at the noise. He nods approvingly and pops on his goggles. The chain splits easily, streaming an arc of blue sparks and smoke. They lift the sandbags and, working against the mud, pull the gate open wide enough to squeeze through. Inside, they feel the texture of cobblelock beneath them. The statue they had seen from the air is now recognisably a stag, standing on a capstone's worth of mountain, antlers wide, chest presenting.

'My monitor's green,' Ram tells them, 'but that still looks like a pit to me, so mask up.'

The brothers comply, strapping their rebreathers over their mouths and noses. Ram approaches the stag and the fountain it's been set in, there is a plaque underneath which reads: *To the god of bad ideas, all my love, Maria.* These words strike Ram as both meaningful and meaningless. He carries on across the yard, disturbing the water and the smells inside it. The monitors stay green, not even blinking yellow in the iffy indecisive way that kept you on your toes, if they're to be trusted, then there's not a trace of gas in the air. All this is bizarre and a little exciting.

Inside the shed, a few loose planks are floating above the pit. Ram has captured a branch of a tree along the way and begins to poke down between the laths, it doesn't even reach three-quarters of its length before he hits the base. His voice adopts a helicopter pilot quality through the mask.

'This isn't even four-foot-deep, and it's just filled up with dirt.'

Breen grabs a handful and lets it glob back down into the water. 'Maybe it was supposed to be a vegetable bed or something?'

'With a forty-foot ceiling?'

Ram feels Lazy's hands coming down gently on his shoulders, massaging affectionate fists into the muscles.

'They probably converted an old cattle barn. Why are you so suspicious of everything?' asks Lazy, finishing with a patriarchal clap on the arms, his eyes on the part of the barn where the generator should be - there's a locked green box there awaiting his attention. He nabs the cold saw from the pocket of Ram's jacket and makes his way over to it.

Breen lifts a pitchfork up out of the water by the spokes and uses it to poke down into the shallow pit.

'Why is this place all walled up, you'd wonder?'

'Family trying to keep it preserved. Some of these estates are here since the plantations, I've seen it before.'

They're interrupted by the squeal of metal being sawn apart.

Lazy is following the seam of the door all the way down below the waterline, leaving an echo of glowing amber in the steel. He uses a crowbar to pull the door open from where the hinges used to be, and it opens back on itself, revealing the generator inside.

Lazy whips round triumphantly. 'What did I say? Does the man do good work?'

Ram gives a long sigh through his nose. 'You got lucky amigo. We'll see how excited you are when we're lugging it, 'cos Chinzer isn't going to be able to airlift that chunk down the road unless we strip it down to dominos.'

Lazy waves away the problem. 'Don't worry about it. We'll get old Marky up that lane, no problema.'

Ram looks back out across the yard at the farmhouse. It's a bit of an eyesore in his opinion, not helped by that stupid statue. Its windows have fake white shutters stuck to the wall on either side, or at least some of them still do. There's a sunroom jutting out oblong from its gable, bay windows plastered up with curtains of eroded plywood. Its fake wood siding gives the building an old world Americana feel, each lath of its once white vinyl now peppered with bulbs of mature moss. It reeks of too much money.

'How about we check the house first and see what we're dealing with? Even if the weather holds, this job will take at least a full day, maybe longer.'

Lazy cocks his head back, staring down at the spaghetti of wires and tubes below the generator. 'Yeah, you're right,' he replies, distracted. 'That's weird.'

Ram is unsurprised, weird is the new normal. 'What now?'

'Ah, nothing crazy, just - can you see where it hits the mains? Looks like it just goes underground.'

Breen tosses the fork into the water.

'Can we still sell it?'

Lazy's beard hides all but the bottom lip of his grin. 'Oh, we can sell the living shit out of it.'

On the way across the yard, Breen takes his phone out to take a picture of the statue, he notices the little red 'x' where the mobile signal should be.

'Coverage is gone.'

Ram closes his visor, the feed says otherwise. 'The drone is picking it up from satellite. Turn your phone off and on again.'

'Mine's gone too,' confirms Lazy. His mask is off now, his unlit pipe gripped between his teeth.

Ram approaches the front door of the house. 'I don't know what to tell ye. I'll check it later.'

They dismantle a mound of sandbags in the doorway and begin to use a crowbar to pry open the lock.

The door lurches open. Water lets itself inside but doesn't get far. All three stand in the doorway, looking gravely at each other. A foot or two inside there's another door, surrounded by the same cavity blocks that extend the perimeter wall. The bolt is locked and chained.

Lazy takes his pipe out of his face and begins to pack it. 'That seems - excessive.'

Ram is having second thoughts about this place. 'Maybe we should just grab the genny and get the fuck out of here.'

Lazy's pocket grows a little lighter. Breen has the saw and is about to decide for everyone. He takes the chain off with one confident drag of the saw, pulls back the lock and opens the door.

'Lowlands are waiting,' he tells them. Ram chastises him with a knuckle-puck right into the bone of his arm. 'It's "lowlands away", you little prick,' he says indignantly, bending down to restack the sandbags so the place doesn't get flooded.

Breen tries his damnedest not to wince, but the steel widgets Ram calls knuckles hurt like a bitch. Lazy steps past them, face focused, eyes probing. *'Lasciate ogni speranza, voi ch'entrate.'*

Breen shoves past Ram, throwing a sly dig down into his ribs.

'What did he say?'

Breen replies in an old-school gangster accent.

'Don'-worry-about-it.'

The air inside smells like someone's left a crate of vegetables rotting under the floorboards, humming up through unventilated carpets soaked and baked dry a thousand times over. As their eyes adjust to the dim light they begin to get a good look at the place, at the once-pearly walls now bruised and ripe with mould colonies an inch deep. There are light switches and dimmers and central heating monitors, all untouched, wires still cosy beneath the plasterboard. There's even some furniture thrown here and there, a delicate table with a broken mirror, a stranded piano stool with an embroidered seat cover, a bench that looks like it used to belong in the garden.

'Ram, this place is the real deal,' says Lazy, eyes still assessing the room.

Ram lays a hand on the banister of the stairs, the steps of which are wide enough to lie across. 'Can't argue with that,' he replies, looking at the worn strip of carpet running up the stairs, 'but someone definitely wants it left alone.'

Breen makes for the kitchen, as if he's picked up the scent of copper pipes through the walls.

'Someone can go and fuck themselves.'

The kitchen is larger than the entire ground floor of Ram's home. There's a sleek kitchen island, large enough to pitch a tent on, housing an enormous marble sink, above it, a wok dangles from a hook. Lazy turns a tap that he's already sold for sixty quid in his head, and the house makes a sound like it's shitting itself before a gloop of tarry fluid flops out of the tap, followed by a dribble of cloudy water. Breen whoops and demands a high-five from Ram, who obliges without eye contact or enthusiasm.

'We'll be gutting her for a week. Fully working plumbing, are you joking me? This is amazing. We are getting paid!'

Ram wanders over to the stove, turns the knob and feels heat and light rush out between the black rings. 'Still got gas over here.' He opens an adjacent cabinet and sure enough the gas canister is standing upright, cushioned by some old shopping bags and a plastic dust pan and brush.

Lazy has opened and closed the fridge, assessing its emptiness. He leans against its double doors contently, relighting his pipe. 'Fuck gutting her, can we just move in? This place is awesome.'

'Nice, all right. Can you imagine having to drop your trousers and walk away from this?'

Breen is hungry for more, his eyes wide and marauding. He wants to know who's coming upstairs with him.

'I'll come. Will you check the rest of the rooms down here?' asks Lazy, addressing Ram.

'Sound out.'

The brothers move out of sight, and Ram turns his attention to a set of double doors in the kitchen. The doors open onto a sunroom, where weathered hickory floors are bubbled to the point of bursting. Papers lie on a pool table, dried brown against the dusty green. There's a rocking horse in the corner wearing a cowboy hat. Ram puts on the hat, thinks he feel fleas nibbling and throws it across the room before heading back through the kitchen.

The hallway is dark save for the few bullet-holes of light raining in from a downstairs bathroom. Inside, there's a cracked toilet bowl, half a dozen plastic razors and some beautifully preserved plumbing. He clips a small flashlight to a strap on his jacket and walks into what he assumes is a closet or laundry room, sure enough, a washer and dryer sit idly against the wall with a pile of black plastic sacks and an old vacuum cleaner for company. This was unprecedented, to find a house left in this condition and not cleaned out. They really had hit a vein in this place, uneasy as he felt about it, a little worm of excitement wriggled in his gut.

This was the kind of vein his father would talk about, back when everything was still fresh and in one piece and newly condemned to the hungry sea, those first seasons when the rinse would leave boats full of technology or drugs, or the bodies of refugees. Back then Mitchelstown was so deep underwater that after the rinse you could boat down and find the carcasses of beached whales and every species of dolphin among the wrecks of helicopters and upside-down traffic.

He rips open a black sack, its gut of women's underwear gathering at his feet. The laundry wouldn't fetch much, but the drums of washing machines alone could fetch anywhere between a hundred and two hundred, depending on the make and model, or they could flog them as fifty-quid fire pits, and that was just the drums. The motor he would keep for Selwyn as payment for Chinny's camera, but on the common market he could easily get a hundred and fifty for this brand.

Mulling things over he makes to leave, his hand already on the doorknob when he's startled by the flash of metal meeting bright light in the dark. His torch settles on flaky, submarine green. There's another door in here: a metal door with long, chunky hinges. He approaches it, hands feeling around the frame where the rough plaster has been hacked at. He knocks on it to hear what it can tell him, solid steel and thick as birch trunk. There's a combination lock in the centre, one of the old analogue ones with the black pins you have to click in the right order.

He foosters around in the dark, searching for the X-ray gun. When he finds it, he places it flat against the steel and swipes at it until something appears. The image on screen is much clearer than that of the tanker, he can see the profile of a banister curling downwards. A basement, he thinks, could even be a bunker if it's combination-locked like this. He experiences a rush of sensory overload. How were they going to gut all this with only the three of them? He would have to be the one to bring it up, of course - the other two knob-ends weren't likely to.

He chews on his prosthetic thumb in the dark, trying to think of another party they could trust enough to share this discovery with. The Callaghans in Bansha, maybe, if they were around. For a vein like this they'd make the time, and hopefully show up with that hovercraft of theirs with its cherry picker. Breen had tapped the younger sister, Theresa, a couple of months back, but it was all above board. This could work. But could it work in a week?

He leaves the room with the door jammed open and heads down the hall, glancing into the living room. There's a three-piece suite in the centre of the room, facing the mark on the wall where a television used to be. A few porcelain trinkets gather dust inside the glass cabinets and the few books that remain are mostly wilted travel magazines or maps from abroad. An old record player on the lowest rung of the bookcase gets Ram down on his knees. The turntable wasn't anything special but styluses were gold dust, you could buy them online but you'd have to borrow a credit card for that, and they took weeks to be delivered. He slides the stylus off the tone arm and turns the player around to find the tiny compartment at the back, then clicks the latch open, sure enough, four needles drop out onto the shelf, still wrapped in plastic.

Delighted with himself, he struts back down the hall, studying the needles in their individual plastic bubbles before funnelling them into his jacket pocket. While his hand is in there he takes out his tobacco and skins. Grinning, still unsure if that feeling in his chest is anxiety or excitement, he begins rolling a cigarette, distilling aromatic tobacco neatly between sheets of sisal skin then licking the edges with the flat tip of his tongue and sealing it with one hand. Holding his disposable lighter up to the light, he discovers the remaining fluid barely meets the lips of the translucent tube within the neon-blue case. He shakes it behind his ear and sparks it a few times until it sustains a steady stump of a flame.

Standing in front of the kitchen, inhaling coarse smoke, he daydreams of coffee with foamy milk, ever so slightly burned in the way he likes it. Suddenly he senses a certain heaviness in the air, a strange orphic stroking of his internal organs that urges him to turn and notice. Upstairs he hears the brothers thumping and dragging things, shouting at each other in Italian. The light in the doorway is changing in real time, clipping, deforming around the edges of something unknown. His eyes adapt to the changing image. A man is standing there.

Chapter 9

Upstairs, the brothers have been in a happy frenzy, ripping light sockets off the walls, pulling fans from the ceilings, tearing up the carpets and the floorboards beneath. They argue briefly about the dismantling of a brass bed before agreeing to work separately. Now Breen is in the hallway discovering the hot press, its interior lined with bare insulation surrounding the immersion cylinder. There's a ribcage of flimsy shelves in front of it, one of them goes over his shoulder and lands down the stairs without his noticing, and the rest he dumps on the floor.

Beneath the orange lagging jacket, the hot-water cylinder is as good as new. Breen lays his forehead against the copper, breathing that smell he loves even more than burning petrol. It smells like blood smells, it smells like money, literally. Lazy leans back against the banister to take a picture and walks right through the frame on his way to the next bedroom. This room has a more modern door handle than the others, cloth-wheel buffed steel, cylinder-locked. He bears down on it but it doesn't budge. Breen passes him the crowbar and he slips it neatly into the door frame.

The man lifts his slim frame over the sandbags, strings of water slapping against the carpet. Ram's chest feels crowded, like it did when he stared into the mouth of the snake. His cigarette is tucked within the cup of his hand, burning slowly against the carbon-fibre palm. He can't stop staring at the stranger's mask, the tight black sheet-rubber that seems sewn to his face, tucked beneath a filthy flat cap. As he approaches, Ram sees his own image deformed in the glare of the wide insect eyes.

The man's hand, with its constellation of visible warts, gropes a series of tubes knotted around the breathing pipe, he pulls the mask up and over his head. Before Ram sees the face, he notices that the man carries no backpack or water. The man's face looks out of place on his skinny frame, swollen, flushed, jowly. His eyes are jaundiced and below the nostrils a millimetre-thick line of red stubble has been missed enough times that it is beginning to curl. Before he speaks, the stranger cocks his head towards the noise from upstairs.

'You shouldn't really be in here,' he says, his tone hinting at crossed territory and impending consequences. 'And they shouldn't be upstairs.'

'Can we help you, buddy?' asks Ram, dragging on his cigarette once more before tossing it into the carpet, showing the man what he thinks of his shitty tone.

'Yeah. You can gather your friends and bring 'em down here, that's what you can do. How many is "we", anyway?'

Authority isn't this man's natural state. Ram smells blood, but isn't sure yet how to treat the guy. He closes the distance between them.

'Listen, pal, if you're staking a claim here you should probably introduce yourself first.' He holds out his hand, watching the squirm in the guy's eye when he notices the prosthetic.

'Name's Ger. You?'

The man seems unprepared for Ram's reaction. It's as if he's done this before but with a different result. Ram is close enough to hear the change in the rhythm of the man's breath.

'I'm the caretaker for this estate, and I'd like to see a piece of paper that says you have a right to be in here.' The crack of a door frame splitting apart causes the man to stop and stare at the ceiling, his jaw visibly tense.

'Paper?' repeats Ram, genuinely perplexed. 'Friend, are you familiar with article 28 of the Constitution? You know, the concept of Inverse Condemnation under Irish law?'

Up on the landing, the bedroom door creaks open into an amber half-light. Lazy squints inside, his eyes struggling to adjust. He can see something in the middle of the room, bathed in the meagre light that has penetrated the boarded window. A smell reaches him, stuffy and antiseptic. Something crumples beneath his feet as he walks inside and he takes a beat to look down, he's walking on translucent sheets of plastic.

'No point in quoting articles at me, I'm getting paid to keep an eye on this land and make sure no looters or squatters get their nippers in, and that's what I'm doing.'

'Well, that's all right because we're neither, and this is new public land. You're going to have to call your employers and tell them to go jump in a fucking puddle, because we're clearing out what we can and coming back for the rest.'

There's a gloss forming on the man's forehead, and his left eye is twitching. 'Nobody wants any kind of trouble. I'm just trying to make myself an honest living. Let's go out into the garden with your friends and we'll discuss it civility...'

The smell is a stench now, overpowering and hostile. In the centre of the room, Lazy lays his hands on what he thinks at first is just a bed. His torch comes on to reveal a mattress which is sectioned into four adjustable pieces. It's not a bed, it's an operating table, he knows this because he's been on one.

At the head of the table a tray extends from a thin cylindrical arm, splattered with what he deduces to be candle wax. He realises what he's looking at and calls for his brother, not realising Breen's already in the room with him, tampering with a cabinet or some sort of unit in the corner. The clatter of heavy rainfall on roof tiles jolts him and then -

'Holy fuck!' shouts Breen, recoiling.

Lazy approaches. The stains are everywhere: on the walls, the floor, the door he's just walked past. He stops beside his brother and shines a beam onto a cluttered workspace. A steel tray flares in the light. Sitting in the tray among the various blades, clamps and instruments are two plastic ziplock bags, they are both filled with what are unmistakably fingers.

Breen grabs his brother's arm. 'Hear that? Is he talking to someone down there?'

Disorientated but lucid enough to feel his heart beating in the crop of his throat, Lazy hears it too - muted tones rising through the floorboards. In this moment he notices two more things: the first is a sealed beaker on the workspace, half-filled with teeth, their gory tails black and dimpled, the second is something which has caught the light from his torch in the ceiling above the door - his eyebrow goes circumflex - he approaches it in a lumbering daze and it winks back at him, sending a cold shiver up through his belly. A pimple of red light blinks beneath the undercarriage of the plastic dome: a security camera.

As Ram speaks the man is wringing his hands, using this pressure to pop the knuckles of his thumbs.

'Look, I can't let you do anything until you speak to the owner. This is part of me livelihood. The nearest phone signal is in the field behind those old stables. You three come out with me and we'll get the owner on the phone. That'll be me covered. Please.'

Ram is about to reply when he twigs. He shoots the man a narrow look. 'I never told you there were three of us.'

The man's eyes suddenly disengage from him, jutting upwards towards the torrent of noise descending the stairs on his right. Lazy appears at the banister with Breen a step behind him.

Each group regards the other and the man speaks first, attempting to take control.

'Afternoon, lads. I'm caretaking this property. We were just talking about going outside to get the owners on the phone.'

The look on Lazy's face, his jaw set behind his twiddled beard, is unfamiliar to Ram. He glances back at the stranger and when his gaze returns to Lazy their eyes meet, obliquely communicating. The man intercepts this look, smiling nervously as he processes it. Suddenly his eye catches the rifle on Lazy's shoulder. The veneer of sweat on the man's forehead has spread out and run down to the soft flesh below his eyes. He rocks back and forth a few times, sniffling, reacting to the tension. Breen shifts his weight on the step and the staircase creaks.

'They're armed.'

The man says this so nonchalantly that it almost doesn't register, then he turns and breaks calmly into a sprint. As if prompted by hunting instinct, Breen vaults the banister and is moving before he even hits the ground. Lazy is faster, he reaches the stranger just as he is about to leap the sandbags. He clamps his arms around the man's legs, bringing them both down into the water. Ram watches all this unfold in a daze, startled by the commotion and the sudden violence. Lazy tosses the man back into the house. His mask has been lost somewhere along the way. He rises and lifts his hands, but Lazy is on him so fast he doesn't even have time to clench his fists.

They land at Ram's feet. 'Fuck it, Lazy, what are you doing?'

Breen stops him from intervening. 'There's something bad upstairs, man. We were coming down to tell you. We've got to go, I mean we've really got to get out of here.'

Lazy has the stranger pinned down, a knee on each shoulder and his rifle hovering above the man's face, 'Who were you talking to, huh? What were you telling them? Who's watching through that camera up there? Speak up.'

'What camera?' asks Ram, trying to keep up.

'There's a kind of torture chamber in one of the rooms upstairs, with cameras and teeth and severed fingers - there's some serious shit going down here, Ram.'

The man is laughing below the gun barrel. Lazy crushes his face into the floor. 'What are you laughing at? You want lead, cunt? You think I won't feed it to you?'

'All right, Luca, relax.' The man keeps laughing. 'You should have come outside with me when I suggested it, Raymond.'

An off-white nub of plastic in the man's ear canal catches Lazy's attention. He reaches down and roughly pops it out, holding it up to the light. The man is hysterical now, howling so hard he begins to cough.

'What is that?'

Lazy can hear low-volume chatter. He slips the earpiece into his ear, the chatter stops for a moment and then a raspy male voice says calmly, 'How's my man doing? You're threatening him.'

Lazy's eyes flare and he gestures to Ram that someone's talking to him. 'Look, we just want to go now, man. No harm done, we didn't see shit, we don't know shit.'

'Go?' There are a number of voices now, laughing in the background. 'Son, where would you go? Look at the weather, catch your death out there. No, you three stay cosy for a while.'

'We're not going to say anything about upstairs. We're just waders, man, looking for copper, we don't know shit about whatever the fuck is going on.'

Lazy listens to breathing and waits for a reply.

'Doesn't sound that way to me, spud. Sounds to me like you know a whole lot more than that.'

'What do you want, man?' Ram turns back towards the door, looking for the source of what sounds like thunder growling, it turns out to be steel, moving.

'St Mark? Patron saint of Venice, am I right? I like that.'

Lazy can hear the same dull laughter rising in the background. 'Stay the fuck away from my boat, dickhead. We've still got your man here, you know.'

Ram watches the first vehicle pull into the drive, an angular multi-windowed chunk of truck with a mudguard as big as a front door. A second, smaller, infantry vehicle rolls in behind it, parched beige in its desert camouflage.

'That's right, you do. Listen, spud, I don't do business over the phone. We'll see you in a minute. If you want this to go smoothly, how about tossing that kiddy rifle out into the garden with your FCA badge? Kisses.'

The line goes dead.

A third vehicle roars into the drive, an armoured truck-boat laid on tank treads with an unmanned machine-gun turret jutting from the top.

Breen jumps the sandbags and shuts both doors, leaning back on them like he's holding back the end of the world.

'What's he saying?'

Lazy stands up, plucks out the earpiece and drops it down on his hostage. 'The line went dead.'

'You're fuckin' antagonising them, Luca.'

'Go and see what's upstairs, fuckhead. They don't need antagonising. And why are you telling him my name?'

'He already knows our bloody names.'

The man on the floor sits back with his arms behind his head, his legs crossed leisurely.

Ram straightens his back, his neck is so stiff he feels it's about to crack.

'I'll go talk to them. This can't be as bad as it looks. We're freaking out, everyone needs to calm the fuck down.'

'There are cut-off extremities floating in jars up there, you feckin' lunatic. How much worse does it have to be? And you're definitely not going out to talk to them. Bree, how many of them are there?'

Breen crouches at the window, peeking out through a hole in the plywood. 'Still in their trucks, but – it looks like one of them is an MRAP with a gun mount. Those things are for warzones, lads, for driving over IEDs and tank mines, what the fuck is it doing in the glen?'

Lazy boots the man in the leg. 'Anything you want to share with us, cunt?'

'No, my job's done, Luca,' the man parries back, enunciating Lazy's real name and grinning smugly.

Lazy stands over him and presses the gun barrel into his forehead, hard enough to leave an impression on the skin.

'This rifle is as old as shit, every time you fire it, the barrel gets hot enough to sizzle in water.' He presses the barrel into the man's cheek this time, producing only giggles. 'You're lucky your daddy's shown up, you little prick, but let me tell you this: if any fuckery goes down, I'm shooting you in the gut first and branding you right there on the forehead with that barrel. I'll brand you right down to the bone so when you wash up a year or ten from now, I'll know who it is before your own mother does.'

The man smiles back at him. 'Ah, you're adorable.'

'What's that, cunt?'

'You think you have a year.'

Ram is by the window with Breen, squinting out through the plywood.

'I'll talk to them from the door. You keep him under control and don't let him get trigger-happy.'

Breen nods back at him, his eyes so wide and white that it ages him in reverse, Ram can see the younger Breen exposed through the stubble and hair and the pockmarks on his neck. He won't admit it, but he is scared underneath it all.

Ram claps him on the arse and winks at him. 'We've been watching too many films. This is blown all out of proportion, wait and see.'

Chapter 10

The rain is playing snare drum on truck bonnets, the three vehicles are idle in the yard, motors running. Several doors open in unison and men, some hooded, step out into the weather. Some are already armed, others make their way to the back of their vehicles to extract their weapons. Two doors remain closed: the passenger sides of the MRAP and the beige transport truck. The MRAP's door sucks open and Mal Dwyer steps out, thick recedes of grey hair netting rainwater. He slips into the driver seat of the transport and closes the door behind him. The mild-faced man he knows only as 'Prester' sits in the passenger seat, clutching a leather satchel, watching the rain swamp the dashboard in a sort of pensive disarray.

'If this isn't cleared up quickly, I'm going to have to inform the man in Paris.'

'Aren't you lucky to have someone to complain to?'

'I told you, you will be compensated for the mistake.'

'You better believe I'll be compensated. If that little girl and her mother bring the army down on me, you'll want me very well fucking compensated.'

'We've been here before: Frankfurt, Maine. We will provide a satisfactory sum, I guarantee that.'

There's a yelping from behind. Mal glances over his shoulder at the Yorkshire terrier in its carrier, yapping at him from the back seat. Its face is trimmed into a near-perfect cube of blonde and black hair.

'Now, the situation at hand - who are they?'

'Three gators from up the road, Christ King. We can see them checking in all over the place, they might as well be pointing an arrow at us. They have my runner, and we don't know who else knows they're here. Probably no one does, but we can't risk it. Once we know for sure, we'll sanitise the situation, which we'd have already done, if your timelines hadn't been so tight between interception and extraction.'

'It was the nature of the operation. The product's location was given to you in real time. It was the extraction of the product which caused the delay.'

Mal reaches beneath his waxed jacket into the shirt pocket beneath and produces a snuffbox. 'They were good men, didn't give up the code until we got right down to the gristle.' He places a pinch of the paprika-coloured snuff on the back of his hand and vacuums it up into his nose. As he does this, Prester notices the faded dots of tattoos on his knuckles.

'Can't we just take the shotgun approach here? This situation is - stressful.'

'Keep your powder dry, Mr Prester. We have to know if someone is going to come looking. This place isn't something you can just cover up with a tarp and leave behind. This all needs to be dealt with professionally.'

'What if someone knows they're here?'

The terrier is still yapping. Mal stares back at it, shooting it a look that he uses to silence men. It doesn't work.

'Then I'm going to be inconvenienced again, aren't I? All because of your sloppy operation. But we're professionals, we'll deal with it. I may have a lady who can take care of the digital footprint.'

'The midden Midwest is going to be an extremely valuable asset now that Nonhoron is under the microscope. The man in

Paris values assets that can deliver.' Prester reaches into his satchel and takes out a dog treat, a slim tube of some brown processed garbage. He reaches back and feeds it through the door of the pen. 'As I say, we have a sum that will satisfy. So if you could get this situation under control quickly, we would appreciate it. I have a flight to catch.'

Mal thumbs his nose, gives Prester a conciliatory nod and exits out into the rain. Closing the door, he pauses and slips the snuffbox back in behind the rows of pens in his pocket protector. The rain rips against the moulded plastic interior of the door.

'One more thing: if we do business again, next time leave your fucking emotional support dog at home. If it gives up my men's position, I'll drown the cute little cunt.'

He slams the door and pulls up his hood. 'Skin!' he shouts, leaning against the boot of the MRAP. A man in a bright blue poncho appears, holding a rucksack and sporting a well-groomed beard. He's young, early thirties. 'Up on that last stable, stay in my ear. Runner 1, same word as last time. Got it?'

Skin nods and breaks away, sloshing off across the yard. Another man, Ryan, arrives at the boot of the MRAP holding a rucksack, which he hands to Mal. Mal peers inside, 'Okay. Once Skin is up there, I'm going to go to the door for the chats. Six-man column at the front of this vehicle and I want two men flanking, Ro and Ger, they know the story.'

Ryan takes a step closer. 'I don't mind being you for this,' he tells him, meaning it.

'It's fine,' replies Mal. 'I'd rather get a feel for it in person. Just keep the column tight and weapons ready.'

Chapter 11

Breen has been staring through the gap in the plywood for so long that it's left an impression on the bridge of his nose. There's movement out there but no faces, just shoulders poking out from behind vehicles, crooked hoods and inaudible chatter.

'What's the story?' asks Lazy, standing by the stairs. The man is sitting on the steps.

Ram's visor shuts. 'I see fifteen, there may be others still in the trucks. Can't go too low, I don't want them to see me.'

'No coverage?'

'It's there, but when I dropped down a little it went again. Anyway, it's not reaching us.' Ram glances over at the man. 'You're blocking the signal, aren't you?'

The man smirks over at him, tonging a fat lip. He gives a goading shrug of the shoulders. Lazy feints a kick at the man, riled by the smug expression on his face. He doesn't flinch, just stares up into Lazy's eyes.

'You'll want to be smart from here on, Luca, put on the big boy trousers.'

Ronan Greene is attaching a tether to his waist while Ryan is standing in front of him relaying orders. Greene is middle-aged and knuckle-bald. His defining feature, a prison swallow tattooed on the back of his head, is drowning in rainwater. He fingers a piece of all-weather plastic on his belt and the barrel-shaped probe responds, floating out from the back seat of his vehicle, hovering silently beside him. The leashed probe is an infantry

Creep, a supply crate designed for carrying military ordnance. A younger man approaches, Ger Boyne, adding a sawn-off shotgun to the pile.

Inside the house, Ram is watching as a line of men spread out in a loose formation in front of the statue in the centre of the yard. A man is approaching.

'Fuck, someone's coming. Keep him quiet and let me do the talking.'

He looks out in time to see the man reach into the rucksack he's carrying. It isn't so much the sock he recognises as the weight inside it, dragging it out of shape.

'You little bastard!' Until now, Ram has been ambling through this situation in a state of conscious denial, this is all just one big misunderstanding. But seeing that gun in a stranger's hand has sucked him into reality like a backdraught. A moment of dizziness passes, replaced by one of suppressed rage.

'What is it?'

'He's got my dad's forty five'

Ram storms towards their prisoner and crouches down in front of him.

'See him?' he asks, pointing to Lazy. 'I know him since I was five. He's all mouth, really, as long as you don't fuck with his brother, you'll be fine. But I am telling you this from the heart, if I don't get that gun back, I am going to stone-cold fucking murder you. I'll do the time, no problem. What'll I get, seven or eight years? Probably be an improvement. Fuck it, I'll row out to Spike Island myself. But I swear to God, I will strangle you under swamp water first...'

A loud rapping is coming from beyond the steel door. Ram kisses his fingers and plants them on the man's forehead.

'You can believe that,' he says, making his way towards the door. He skips over the sandbag. The water is cold, particularly at his ankles. He takes a breath and then another. The gun is making him irrational, he tries to steady himself, but his chest is pumping vinegar. He cracks the door open a few inches, clears his throat then shouts out, 'This is a lot of drama for nothing, friend. You've got no problem with us.'

The front door opens, as it does, Ram closes his own door a notch more. The new man's profile slides out from behind the door frame, he's leaning back against the outside wall, using the concrete for cover.

'How is my man doing? You treating him right?' This man's voice is gravelly and eerily calm. Through the empty doorway Ram sees the line of armed men, behind them the statue, and behind that the whole wide world.

'He's fine, nothing a few pints won't fix.'

'Who am I talking to?' asks the new man, holding out three ID cards and the tax relief documentation Ram had stored in his backpack. 'Raymond, Luca, Breen?'

'Don't appreciate you going through our stuff, man. Don't like that one little bit.' Ram wants to mention the gun, but he doesn't. The worst thing you can do with a bully is to let them know they've got something you want.

'The feeling is mutual, spud.' The sparking of a lighter precedes a flume of cigar smoke from the edge of the doorway. 'Okay, let's get this over with and maybe we can all get in a few jars afterwards. Christ knows it's a day for the high stool.'

Ram takes a glance back at Lazy. Breen is to his right, his face one big worried wrinkle. 'Okay. What have you got in mind?'

The man's hand bobs in the doorway, his cigar rolling back and forth between his fingers.

'Well, here's the thing. We had a job the other night, a couple of shipments came in, no need to say what. We bumped into a few unfriendlies and one of my boys caught a lead sliotar, lost himself a few fingers. We had to operate on him upstairs, hence the mess which your friends there traipsed through, spreading evidence all over the fucking place.'

'Sounds like something that'd make the news.'

'Does, doesn't it, Raymond?'

'Name's Ram. That man of yours okay? No bodies buried in the walls?'

'I'm Malik, by the way, call me Mal. Yeah, he's fine, won't be playing poker for a time, but he wasn't much good anyway.'

'Sounds like a victimless crime to me. No moral obligation on us to go to the authorities, we're not their biggest fans anyway and as you can imagine they ain't ours either. Let's get that out in the open right away.'

'Good. Fuck pigs, we're all in agreement. Dandy. Now, I get the feeling we understand one another, Ram, and that's very positive, but you have to see things from my perspective. We can trust you three but we have to know who else is in the loop. Anyone else know you're here? Has anyone been and gone since you arrived?'

'Well, maybe that's information I should keep to myself for now.'

'Okay, I get it. Smart move. You're staring down a line of men armed to the teeth and need to keep what leverage you have. How about we all drop the weapons and you come on out, and we'll talk this over like men? You have to understand, my man in there told us you were armed, thought the unfriendlies had come back for the rest of us, so we had to come prepared. And look, I'm a businessman, I know walking away from this place will cost you. I'm sure we can work something out.'

'That's very reasonable, Mal, but how about I save you some

money, we just want to walk away. So how about you bring our boat and all our stuff up into the drive, then we come out with your man, drive off and leave him down the lane. You'll never see or hear from us again.'

'Now, Ram, you're not thinking laterally. You can't think in black-and-white here, it's not a black-and-white situation. If you go, then we've got no assurances and we spend the rest of our lives worrying you boys will find Jesus and have the law on us. Why would we do that?'

Lazy is getting twitchy, sweating below his eyelids. He has the feeling Ram is being played along. 'Because that's what's going to happen, fuckface!' he shouts. 'We're not negotiating. Get my fucking boat up here without a scratch on it, now!'

Puffs of rusty smoke drift silently into the brace of the doorway. Ram's stump is beginning to itch from sweat, right down to the dry socket.

'Wow,' says Mal finally. 'I don't think your friend there understands your situation, Ram. Your plan isn't very long-sighted. I'm holding all the cards here, not to mention the guns. Now, say I do let you go.'

Mal flicks open a sheet of paper and holds it out so Ram can see it. 'What's stopping us sneaking in to 11 Pearse Street, Christ King and making sure that you and yours sleep through a chip-pan fire, or a monoxide leak? See, it's best we come to a more amicable agreement here based on trust, money and a little trouser-shitting fear, man to man.'

Given half a chance, Ram could burst into tears right now. It was likely he already had. This man, whom he can't get a clear look at, this stranger with his battalion of men and guns has just kicked in the door to his private life: his dad's gun, his mother's house. Ram is frightened. He's not sure he can speak without stuttering. 'Look, Malik, your boy in here's been making threats like that for the last hour.' Ram swallows, afraid to blink in case a tear rolls out. 'They're not working on us.'

'They work on the mouth back there, 'cus he calls me 'fuckface' again-' interrupts Mal.

'Don't worry about him, you're talking to me. He's right, though, we're not coming out unless the boat is in the drive, and your man isn't either. You're not going to start shooting the place up while he's in here, so go fetch our boat and let's get this done.'

'What in fuck happened to you, Ram?' Mal's tone has changed, the pitch of his voice is lower. 'What kind of a smack did you take to the head to make you think you can tell me what to do?' Mal walks out to stand in the doorway. He's in his late fifties, with ashen hair slicked back up over his scalp and overgrown, droopy ears.

Instinctively Ram closes the door, and shouts through it. 'If you want your man back safe, you'll bring that boat up.'

'Nah, I don't think I'm going to do that, spud.'

'Just get us the boat, man. It's going to be dark soon, and you've got a bunch of lads out here in the rain for nothing. We get the picture: you mean business, you've got guns. We're not saying shit to anyone.'

'You know, I still don't think you do. Skin, show 'em the picture. Saltpetre on one.'

Before he has any context for it, before he even hears the noise or notices the slim channel of light burn through the room, Lazy is pulling pieces of something out of his beard. The clumps are silky, and warm and jagged, like pieces of salmon with the bones still inside. He wills himself to look. Information is flowing in but being processed non-linearly, he's seeing images that don't yet make sense. Then, all at once, they make perfect sense.

The man is still perched on his step, third from the bottom, his head in his hands, when he lifts it he is missing the quadrant of skull directly above his left eye. Blood ribbons from his nose down into his hands and right through his fingers. He tries to stand, but only one leg is kicking. Finally he collapses into a seizure, flopping around at the bottom of the stairs.

Lazy looks to Ram for answers. Breen is in his peripheral, face draining to translucence. Ram offers only a slack, empty expression, his ears are ringing, his stomach is clenched tight and in need of evacuation. Below, the man whose name he never learned shudders to his death on the floor, while beyond the steel door Mal is speaking. His tone is calm, chummy and terrifying.

'Gone quiet on me, Ram? Let me tell you a story that might help you get your thoughts in order. In 1641, Oliver Cromwell rides into Drogheda. Winter at his heels. He needs the port towns to keep his army of cunts fed and watered for the months ahead, but the garrison in Drogheda is held by good men, brave men, Irish and English. Cromwell sends in a note, the wording of which I used to be able to recite by heart, let me see if I can remember some of it for you.'

Mal leaves a pause while he puffs and ponders. Inside, Lazy goes to his brother's side, lays his hand on his shoulder and stares into his eyes, a mute guarantee that everything is going to be all right.

Mal clears his throat and puts out his cigar against the door-frame.

'Having brought the army of the Parliament of England before this place, to reduce it to obedience, to the end that the effusion of blood may be prevented, I thought fit to summon you to deliver the same into my hands to their use. If this be refused, you will have no cause to blame me. What a way to put it! Surrender, or don't blame

me for what I'm going to do. He was a man of his word, Ram. The brave men of Drogheda told him to go fuck himself, of course, so he stormed the breach, clubbed those men to death and lined the road to Dublin with their battered heads. Now take a moment to think, will you? Look into the crater where my man's face used to be and ask yourself: if that's what he'd do to a man who worked for him, a man who allowed himself to be put in a hostage situation, then what the hell might he do to three little who-the-fuck-cares from the back-arse of nowhere. Then get yourselves out here as quick as you can , before you get yourselves reduced to fucking obedience.'

Ram feels a tug at his shoulder and all at once he's in a huddle, trying to listen but unable to avoid staring at the dead body, fingers twitching, still in spasm. Within the sights of an infrared scope, the lads appear as a single mercurial organism.

'They're talking it over,' Mal hears through his earpiece. Breen is swallowing air too fast and looks as though he's on the very edges of a panic attack. Ram tries to speak first, but Lazy cuts him off.

'We can't go out there. They'll fucking kill us.'

Ram checks his phone again, still nothing. 'What do we do, then?'

'Run?' Breen manages. 'Can you video them with the drone and fly it to Nursery or home or somewhere?'

'We don't have the time, man. We either trust them or- there's a basement, back there in the laundry room. There could be something down there, a landline or a computer. If they were watching us from outside the house, they must be broadcasting to somewhere.'

The thought of a dark basement is turning Breen's stomach.

Mal's voice booms in the doorway. 'Counting to ten, lads.'

‹The basement's our only option.› Ram states it as a fact.

'Three . . . '

'Jesus,' whispers Lazy.

'Nine . . . ah, fuck it, I tried.'

What happens next happens quickly. The first shot Mal fires ricochets off the steel door and sends a piece of cinder-block spinning back over his shoulder. All at once a torrent of automated gunfire bombards the house, shattering glass and timber, sending chipboard and plaster whizzing around the hallway. In unspoken unison, Ram, Lazy and Breen bolt towards the kitchen, the walls spitting chalky clouds around the corridor as they move. Something punches Ram in the shoulder, knocking him into a waddling gait, he manages to get through the kitchen door and down onto his knees. Turning, he sees Breen reach down to grab his brother by the scruff of his collar and drag him through the doorway.

The rifle has been left behind. Ram dives for it, sliding across the tiled kitchen floor. He gets a hand on it, holds it to his chest and turns to crawl back when it registers that the ring finger of his prosthetic has been shot clean off, along with the tip of the index digit.

Once inside he and Breen close the door, and between the two of them they position the fridge across the doorway. They get behind the kitchen island where Lazy is already sitting, staring down at the flap of meat that used to be his knee. The house sounds as if it's being torn apart a quarter of an inch at a time. The single pot hung above the island clanks off its hook and lands between Ram's legs, the fright makes him throw it away, as if it's a dead rat that's just fallen from the ceiling. Before the pot has finished rattling on the floor the gunfire stops, leaving nothing but the breathy calm of rain falling.

Ram discovers that he has the constitution to act, so he does, turning to Lazy who is now bleached white and soaking in sweat. Ram takes the tub of medical putty from his jacket pocket, but he can tell it's empty by the weight of it. He reaches into Breen's inside pocket and pulls out the length of hosepipe he'd used to suck the gasoline from the motorbike. Breen barely reacts, he isn't sobbing but his cheeks are damp and mottled, and when Ram grabs his face and shakes it a tear rolls down.

'Are you hurt?'

'No.'

'Double check,' Ram tells him, moving over to Lazy.

He looms above the leg, trying not to look directly into the wound.

'I need something like a penknife, or that comb you use.'

Lazy looks at him in confusion, swallowing incessantly as if he's fighting off the urge to vomit.

'Bree, take off your jumper, vest, socks - anything, and start cutting them up.'

Breen complies automatically, pulling his jumper up over his head, straps and jacket still attached. Ram plucks the beard comb from Lazy's jacket pocket and puts it between his teeth. He reaches for Lazy's leg, but as he does, Lazy grabs both his hands. 'Don't! Just leave it. Please don't touch it. It's not that bad.'

Ram replies through the comb in his teeth. 'All bleeding stops eventually, man. Either I stop it, or it stops the other way.'

Lazy takes a long stiff breath through the nostrils and as he does Breen's hand finds the back of his neck. It's cold and moist. Lazy sets his jaw, and with both hands he grabs his brother's wrist. 'We're fine. I'm fine. Don't be scared.'

Breen smacks his hands away. 'I'm scared because you've a hole in you. Stop being a puss and let him plug it.'

Lazy straightens his back against the island, eyes loosely shut, he nods at Ram to go ahead. Ram nods back at him. 'Give me your shoelaces, I'm going to tie it up. Breen, as soon as I start twisting, start stuffing both sides of his knee then tie it all up with that length of hose.'

Breen holds out the rags of his jumper as if he's getting ready to pounce on an animal. Ram carefully wraps the laces above the knee, tying both ends into a half-knot then pulling them tight enough to make Lazy suck in air through his teeth. 'This is going to hurt, have you something to bite down on?'

Lazy reaches into his coat pocket and pulls out a tattered notebook, folds it over and feeds it between his teeth. Ram slides the comb into the knot and takes a deep breath, gives Breen a look that says, 'You'd better be ready,' and begins to turns the comb like he's tightening a valve.

Chapter 12

Mal's closed fist is still in the air when Prester descends from the vehicle, the dog's histrionic yapping cut off by the door slamming shut behind him. Prester unfolds a small umbrella and holds it above his head and hunched shoulders. The water is an inch below his knees, almost twice the depth it had been when they arrived. He wades clumsily towards Mal, who has his finger in his ear, talking to someone.

'Is it sorted out?' Prester shouts.

Mal stares at him as if he's just walked in on him taking a shit. 'Why are you outside?'

'The shooting stopped. I thought it was over.' Prester squints at the house as if he's expecting to see something. 'Are they still in there?'

'This old house has a bit more give to it than we thought. We dinged two of 'em, but they've retreated into the back. It's no problem, just a few more minutes.'

'It's a lot of noise, Mal.'

Mal throws out his arms theatrically. 'What do you want me to do, blow darts at them?'

'I have a flight to catch.'

'Get back in that fucking truck!' Mal holds back the rest, but his eyes articulate the sentiment.

Ryan approaches, swapping over a magazine. Prester turns to leave, looking hurt, and for a fleeting moment Ryan considers a friendly shoulder-bump, just hard enough to let him know what's what.

'Who are we sending in?' asks Ryan. 'I'm up for it.'

'Hold back for a minute. You rush in now while they're skulling adrenaline you'll give 'em an edge, somebody's likely to get hurt. Give them a second to bleed, to think about never seeing mammy again. A few minutes of that, and nine times out of ten they come out by themselves. In the meantime pick a partner, use a mix of smoke and flash bangs. Ro and Ger should be at the flank. Skin says they've barricaded themselves in the kitchen.'

'Will I get Fred set up?'

'We brought Fred?'

'Think so, yeah. Didn't unpack him last time.'

The conversation is interrupted by a short guttural roaring. They turn and stare back into the doorway. Ryan raises an eyebrow at Mal, who is listening for an encore. Sure enough, another noise emerges from the pores of the house, this time a series of panting howls.

'God damn, I remember the last time I made that noise,' Says Mal, tipping some fresh snuff out onto his knuckles. Ryan detects a hint of sympathy in his voice.

'They could have done it the easy way.'

'Would you have?'

'Fuck, no.'

Mal licks the back of his hand where the snuff and the rain have formed a bitter paste. He hocks it all together and spits out the result. 'All right, ten minutes, then it's surgery. Go see if Fred's got enough juice in him for a barricade, and kick those sandbags out, I want them bleeding in floodwater.'

Chapter 13

Ram's hand is holding the comb steady, preventing the fertile tracts of Lazy's veins from emptying themselves all over the tiled floor. Ram's holding the comb in place because Lazy can't, he's passed out against Ram's chest, face mushed against his shoulder. Ram holds him in a motherly grasp, arm around his shoulders. He stretches out his hand and regards the few fingers he has left on it. To his amusement, he catches himself worrying about how much this going to cost him. These things aren't cheap, but he needs his fucking hands for laying fibre. It occurs to him, passively, that he's already decided this situation will not be the end of him.

Breen feels the water swamping in around them.

'They've taken down the sandbags.'

'They're fucking with us. This crowd know we have at least one gun, and they don't know who else might know we're here. So, they'll be wanting at least one of us alive so they can pull our teeth until we tell 'em.'

'That's why they've stopped shooting?' says Breen.

'Yeah.'

Breen is past being terrified, he's acclimatising to it. Now he's just angry. 'If I hear them at that door, I'm putting a bullet through it.'

'Not with my gun, you're not.' Lazy comes to, pale and squinting. 'Nobody's shooting them cunts but me.'

'You can't even open your eyes. Just sit back and don't bleed to death,' Ram tells him, helping him to sit up straight.

Lazy rifles through his pockets, eyes still wandering vacantly, he finds the small loop of insulation tape, takes it out and holds it up to his face. 'That fucking hurt, man. Jesus!' he announces.

'Kissing it better wasn't an option. You could have told us you had that before you fainted.'

'I didn't faint, gringo, I blacked out from the pain.' Straining forward, he surveys his knee. 'Hold that thing steady for me.'

Lazy tapes the comb into place, fingers shaking, caked with mud and gore. He wraps it a few more times to make sure it's tight, and then does the same with the hose. A wedge of board sags from the window-frame above the kitchen sink and through it the sky is visible, full of patient candyfloss clouds. It's nearly dark.

'Did you two come up with a plan while I was out?' Lazy asks, gesturing for his rifle. Breen hands it to him.

He puts the tape in his mouth, cocks the gun so the magazine drops out and begins removing ammunition from his chest strap.

'The way I see it," Ram replies, 'they should have just strafed the house with that machine gun, soon as they pulled in, but they didn't, so whatever they're into, they gotta make sure there aren't any loose ends. That's our only advantage, so way I see it, our only plan is getting downstairs. If we go out that window or through the sunroom, we'll get out of the house all right but we won't get clear. Even if we got far enough to get a mobile signal it'd be a long time before anyone got here, too long to be out in the open. I say we make a stand until they make another move. Make ourselves more hassle than we're worth and wait till we get a clear path to the laundry room.'

'That door you found, suppose it's locked?' asks Lazy, now jungle taping magazines together, two at a time.

'We'll frost it.'

'Okay, I'll get behind that, but you know once we get down there we're going to be in the same position as we are now.'

'They've got something down there, man. You don't carry this kind of artillery around for nothing. They've got drugs or weapons or something down there, something we can use as leverage. Plus I fucking know they have communications, they must do.'

'Okay. Well, what weapons we got?'

'I've got my small axe, Bree has a machete, we've got the saw, then there's the crowbar, penknife, hands, feet, teeth. Are you sure you've got it in you to use that thing on a person?'

Lazy snaps the magazine back into the belly of the rifle. 'You fuck with my Mam not seeing her boys again, you don't get to be a person no more. Let's raise some welts on these pricks.'

Chapter 14

The hood of Ronan Greene's poncho keeps creasing itself into kettle spouts and tipping rainwater down his face. The side of the house is an overgrown lawn, plagued with a generation's worth of weeds and making it difficult to navigate with any degree of stealth. An antique swath turner sits in the lawn, rusty frame decorated with the purple bells of ling heather and bog cotton, all bowing west in the wind. Ger is just ahead of him, peeping around the corner of the house, checking the back garden. No visible signs of escape, no kicked-out windows or bloody debris, just the loud knocking of water pouring from a battered gutter onto the canopy.

'Back way looks clear,' Ger whispers to the air. 'They seem to be still inside.'

A loud wheezing starts and he turns around, startled, SMG at his shoulder, elbow tucked beneath the barrel. A stream of pale smoke burbles out the plastic flue and ballerinas off into the wind. Ger thumbs the safety catch and checks his watch.

'Fuck me,' he says, relieved. 'Downstairs boiler comes on when it gets too cold down there.'

Ronan wipes his face nervously. 'You scared the living shit out of me.'

Ger acknowledges the mistake with a nod, then taps the mike in his ear. 'We're going to get into position behind the kitchen window. You say when, boss.'

'Another minute or two. Hang tight,' Mal replies on his way to the truck. At the side of the vehicle, Ryan is operating the lift, a torch shining between his teeth. The lift brings the gadget down into the water. Ryan unzips the plastic cover, folds it half-neatly and tosses it back into the truck. He squats down and plays with a control panel on the machine, then suddenly the hunk of metal lurches forward, unfolding its limbs and standing upright. Fred is a Swedish-built, six-foot-three Band Leader bot or Arbetare. Its shoulder hydraulics are above industrial standard, and its bright blue body is badged all over with republican paraphernalia and football stickers. Its head is a panelled rectangle with a spherical visual system onto which someone has painted a happy face.

'I don't suppose you can strap a fifty calibre to him yet,' quips Mal.

'Have you a couple of million to spare for a new chassis?'

Mal pats Fred on the back. 'I wouldn't do that to you, Freddy, don't you worry.'

Ryan slides open a panel on Fred's chest and holds his wrist to the scanner beneath. A low beep acknowledges the pairing with his wrist strap. Next he takes a slip of paper-thin plastic from his inside pocket and unpeels the Cog dots. He sticks most of them to his temple and one behind his right ear. Ryan performs a number of operational tests: he raises Fred's arms, makes him take a step back and then to one side. Finally he cogs a high-five that ends with a thumbs-up. Mal approves.

'Bringing Richie in,' Ryan tells him. 'Any trouble, I'll signal to Ger and Ro. I'll try and keep one alive.'

'No need to take chances, just get it done, neat and tidy.'

Chapter 15

It isn't until Ram begins to move him that Lazy realises he has shat himself, that shameful peeling feeling in the back of his pants. They lock eyes at the ripe pong, both equally disgusted. Ram positions him on the ground to the left of the sink, giving him a clear view of the kitchen door at just enough of an angle to give him cover behind the island if he needs it. Two cupboard doors Ram has pulled from their hinges keep Lazy's leg above the waterline.

Breen has been delegated to add bulk to the barricades, stacking whatever he can get his hands on in front of the two doors. The plan is for Breen to cover the left, tucked into the corner, this is deemed the safer of the two sides, partly because his brother is covering that side with his rifle but also because there is a second doorway to be covered on the other side, the sunroom door. They take up their positions.

Between the dark, the rain and the strengthening gale Ram is finding it hard to see anything through Chinny's camera, but he sees enough. The dogfight in his chest begins to escalate. He notices movement by the front door: one of the trucks changing position, faint heat signatures skipping in and out of the gloom. He snaps the visor closed and slaps his ear to the wall, mechanical noises, sloshing water, wind, rain and whispers. They ready themselves as best they can and await whatever is coming.

A set of white goalposts wilted into a triangle still stands in the back garden, several acres of sloping, wild allotment sprouting from the nape of the house. Ger and Ronan wait by the porch in the twilight, unwilling to climb the veranda for fear the boards will creak and alert the enemy. Orders are flowing into Ger's ear from the front of the house, he leans attentively and then turns back to Ronan to relay them. He lifts two fingers, then gestures that they should move around to the veranda steps. Ronan nods, letting Ger lead the way. Ger moves, slow and crouched and steady. Ronan tries to follow, and then he tries harder. He can't get his right leg out of the mud.

He straps his sub-machine gun around his shoulder, reaches down and tries to free the leg, but it's not budging, in fact it's getting tighter. Ger notices and turns back to see what's causing the delay.

'What's wrong?' he whispers frantically.

'I'm stuck!' Ronan spits back. Ger wades over, lets Ronan grab him for leverage and then tries to pull him free. Mal is in his ear: one minute to breach. He hands Ronan his SMG and reaches down between his legs, cheek to cheek with the waterline. He fingers something thick and cold and heavy, tries to lift it with one hand and then two, teeth clamped, jaw tensed. It gives a little. He reaches down again, deeper this time, as deep as he can. The water begins to gyrate, gathering up beneath them. Ger reaches for his torch and holds it close to the water, before he even thumbs the spongy switch something has him by the throat.

Ronan witnesses it, the raw kinetic strike, the strength of it, the patterns of its skin, he's seeing images that don't make sense. And then all at once they make perfect sense. Ger can't scream, the snake's teeth are pinned into every muscle of his throat. The best he can produce is a loud bubbling wheeze.

Ronan's legs are crushed together at the knees. He fumbles for his gun, finds it, cocks it, points it down into the water and fires wildly. Ger watches him all the while, his hands wrung around the reptile's head, trying to rip it off. A hot jet of blood hits his chin and steams in the cool air. Struggling only makes the teeth sink deeper. He punches at the snake, but by now the punches are so weak they're almost affectionate. He hears shots in the near distance and small things pass through his abdomen. Mal is shouting in his ear. Unsteady now, he sees Ronan's head buck from a bullet. Ger closes his eyes. It is warm and familiar.

Lazy throws himself off the kitchen sink, the pain less important than his excitement. 'Head shot!'

Ram is still cringing from the gunshots. 'Are you fucking serious? You are, aren't you? You just killed somebody.'

'They fired first. Geneva convention or some shit.'

'Jesus,' says Breen.

'We should have blocked that window. I got it open too easily.'

Through the walls Ram hears a commotion - Mal's croak of a voice grinding out orders. What follows isn't clear, a heavy sloshing, and then what sound like an iron door being torn off its hinges. Ram stares across the barricade to Breen, his hair in a bun, his cheeks pumping stiff breaths through cracked lips.

'Get ready.'

Fred's fist smashes through the solid pine door, sending chips and dust pistoling through the air. Immediately Lazy starts firing, cracks of semi-automatic fire meeting the dull thump of bullets hitting impenetrable steel. The arm reaches through, all the way up to the shoulder, turning 180 degrees clockwise and grabbing a fistful of the wall above the doorway. The room shudders. A flurry of gunfire passes through the door in Lazy's direction, but between Fred, the door, the barricade and the island it doesn't reach him.

The arm disappears back into the hallway, bringing with it a chunk of door and wall. Fred has been manufactured to manipulate objects of solid dimensions, skips filled with building materials, quarry carts or steel beams, not threaded stone and plasterboard.

A moment passes.

The arm enters again and repositions, this time rotating in Breen's direction, reaching over and grabbing the fridge which creases like bedsheets. Breen drops the machete, unclips the saw and goes to work on the arm. Lazy provides cover, sending semi-automatic rounds whistling across the kitchen and into the hallway. Finger-length sparks flow across the barricades in a bright handsome arc. Breen feels the blade hit something soft and the arm yanks away through the slot in the doorway, its limp forearm flopping from the elbow joint.

The descending sound of machinery gives them brief hope that their assailants might be in retreat. Three shells fly through the room, whizzing smoke trails as they go.

'Masks!' cries Ram, reaching for his rebreather. Before he knows what's coming, he's thrown by a concussive slap to the wall behind him. He gets to his feet, the pall of smoke swallowing him and everything else. Another crash shakes him. They're ramming the doorway. He's temporarily blind.

It's the third crack that tells him they're in. He feels for the kitchen island behind him, using the corners of the countertop to create some semblance of situational awareness. A faint figure emerges from the static, rushing towards the island. He's going for Lazy. Ram gores him like a bull, shouldering him off balance and into the mist. As he turns to go back to his corner of the counter he sees a second man mounting the island. They know Lazy has the only gun, they're trying to kill him first.

He scrambles across the counter. Ryan sees him, raises his

weapon to fire. Still on the counter, Ram reaches out and grabs the barrel, forcing it up and clear. It fires anyway, close enough to deafen him. He's never been deafened before, it's exactly as he would have expected: the ringing, the tension in his temples. Ram can smell his prosthetic burning, he can tell it's been shot apart, that the thumb and little finger are the only things stopping the gun from coming loose. Then he remembers what's in his other hand. His axe finds the man's shoulder. The shooting stops.

Ryan dives on top of him, trying to wrestle the gun out of Ram's hand while defending himself from the axe. They tumble to the ground on the other side. Their positions change, Ram is on top and in control. He lifts the axe, intentions set on the man's head. Ryan drops the gun altogether and reaches to grab Ram's hand on its way down. He assesses his strength and almost laughs at how little effort it takes to hip-flick him to one side.

They both rise. Ryan pulls off his mask and tosses it into the thinning smoke. A screaming from somewhere draws Ram's attention for a second too long. Ryan takes advantage, striking fast and surgically. Ram is rocked by a right hand, may even have blacked out for quarter second. The axe isn't in his hand anymore and, as he looks down to find it, Ryan takes his back, locking him into a rear-naked choke. One alive, just like he promised the boss.

Ram feels an immense pressure between his shoulders, forcing him down to his knees. Legs coil around his abdomen, locking into a triangle. It's not his choice to lie back into the man's chest, it's happening whether he likes it or not. Ram is being dismantled, professionally. The pressure is building, his tongue feels too big for his mouth, his forehead is about to split like a melon.

All the while Ryan is whispering, 'Go to sleep, go to sleep.'

Ram's back arches involuntarily, he's going to black out or

explode, or both. His legs are flailing in the water, his vision is getting spotty and weird. He senses himself slipping away, like he could reach out and touch unconsciousness. The ringing in his ears is fading. Before the warm blanket of unconsciousness finds him, Ram has an awareness of something. Something angular poking him, jabbing him in the kidneys. He remembers what it is and a rush of excitement builds, a last jolt of adrenaline.

He reaches for it, wrestles with the clasp and pulls it loose. He fingers the trigger and a little frost spits out from the foam gun, and onto his chest. He knows by the weight of it that it's not empty. Ram stabs it upwards and pulls the trigger. The foam spreads across Ryan's face, up his nose, into his mouth, his eyes. Ryan almost giggles, wondering what the hell this shit is. He squeezes as hard as he can.

'Go to fucking sleep, you little prick,' he barks, spittle and foam lancing from his mouth.

Ram summons whatever energy he has left and pushes back, leaning into Ryan's grip, shoving his head up under Ryan's chin and simultaneously thrashing up water with the palm of his prosthetic. He hears the sound: the hissing they add in manufacturing, along with that chemical smell. You shouldn't hear this sound from closer than a metre and a half, like it says on the back of the pack.

And then he's free, coughing up phlegm as thick as tile grout, but free all the same.

Ryan is wailing like a toddler, his face is being bitten off, chemically, flaking apart in his hands. Ram feels it too, a nice big blob of foam has landed on his forehead and in his hair. He ignores it, turns and mounts Ryan's chest and with what's left of his carbon-fibre hand, he grabs Ryan's face and drives it down into the water. It's a piranha-feeding frenzy, a wild chemical boiling below him. Some loose specks of frost start burning his cheeks and chin, tiny little pinholes of intense pain that he has to ignore for a little longer.

He feels his hand slip deeper, past bone. The thrashing stops Ryan's skull collapses, it feels like Ram has squashed an Easter egg. All around him the water turns lumpy and dark. He lifts his prosthetic out of the gore, nothing left below the wrist but twisted gristle. Around him, the smoke is turning pale and fine. He lifts his shaking hand towards his face. A pea-sized piece of petrified flesh falls from his nostril. He tastes blood in his mouth. He doesn't want to think about what the frost has done to his face.

He hears Lazy's voice shouting something in Italian. Two shots ring out. A man stumbles in from the mist, masked in a balaclava and dressed in black. The man is clutching his stomach. His eyes lock onto Ram's, then he falls face down into the water and following him down is Breen, wielding his machete. He strikes him viciously, so deep that the blade catches and he has to wrench it back out with both hands.

Breen is feral now, blood spattered all up his face. He ends it with one great stab into the back of the man's head, leaving the blade standing upright like a chef does after a filleting. Ram watches him do it, unable to see it as anything else but a spectacle. Some sort of real-as-life performance being played out in front of him. Only it's not like television, it's quick and real, and he can smell it. Breen lets out a scream, right down into the thing he's just murdered. He's got the man's gun now, and stands up like he's waiting for his applause. He's survived the damnation to beasts and wants the emperor to know, so he unloads a magazine out into the hall.

Out in the yard, men scatter for cover. A bullet finds a man's shinbone, another drives a crack into the windscreen of the

MRAP, sending Prester curling beneath the dashboard.

Mal is using the statue for cover, down in the water up to his chest. Breen's profile lights up like he's sweating out sunset.

Skin takes his shot. Three in the chest, one in the throat. If Ram hadn't thrown himself onto him, it would have been a head shot. It didn't matter, he was suffocating before he hit the floor, dying before his brother ripped open his shirt.

Gone.

Chapter 16

Skin reloads and relays what he knows into his earpiece. 'I got one.'

Mal stands up out of cover, flummoxed, confused at what's just played out.

'One? Are you fucking joking me? Where are the other four? Ger? Ro? Richie? Ryano, what's the situation?'

No answer.

Skin tells him, 'He was using one of our guns, the guy I just starched. I think ... I think they took 'em out, boss.'

Mal looks around, communicating a question silently to the world, What in the name of Christ just happened?

The door of the MRAP creaks open. Prester limps out, his face mottled with tears. He's holding his arm.

'I'm hurt,' he weasels out. The dog somewhere, yapping. He was hurt, a bullet must have passed through the vents at the front of the truck. 'I've been shot. Am I going to die? I don't want to.'

Mal watches him, more curious than concerned, some medical putty and he'll be fine. Christ knows how he's going to spin this.

A noise draws Mal's attention: a low buzzing like the rotary blades of a distant helicopter, but they don't fly in this weather. He watches the sky, Prester still moaning behind him. The first stars are appearing in the deep indigo beyond the clouds. The noise has a direction but there's nothing visible there, then he sees the ignition of fuel, the bright tail.

Skin notices it too. He kneels up from his position, prone on top of the corrugated roof. He squints at the thin, smoke bellowing thing approaching. The drone passes through him just below the ribcage. As Skin slides off the roof, leaving a shiny trail behind him, Selwyn's premonition comes true, just like Ram knew it would. Selwyn knows his shit, always has done.

Chinny barrels through the air, whirling over the heads of Mal's men, lances itself into the side door of one of the vehicles and explodes impressively.

Mal dives for cover underneath the water, where for a moment he finds calm. It's at this moment that his responsibilities reach him. Richard Gleeson has a son and a fiancée, Ronan Greene a father with bowel cancer. Mal's not sure he wants to get back up again.

His knee pops, like it's done since he was twenty. Flames lap the truck. One of his men, Burgess, is being patted down with someone's jacket. Then he hears Prester, screaming like a fox at midnight.

Prester has flames on his shoulders, fuel or oil has landed on him and he's burning, smashing himself off the hood of the truck to try to quench it. Mal finds it very hard to feel sympathy for a man who tries to beat a fire out on aluminium when he's knee-deep in water. He smells hair burning and thinks of Paris. There's going to be no way to spin this. He approaches Prester from the rear and fires one clean shot into the back of his head, then tucks the gun away in his pocket as if to deny what he's just done. One of his men appears beside him, baby-faced, terrified.

'What do we do now?' the man asks.

Mal doesn't answer immediately, just kicks water absently over Prester's smouldering corpse. He turns away and rests his finger on his top lip, faint traces of snuff still emanating from his fingernails. He tells himself that his responsibility now is to his remaining men. The men understood the risks, cruel necessities of the work. They trusted him to get them out of this shit, and he would. This problem can be resolved like anything else. He just needs to remain calm, stays the course. In times of chaos, lean back on your training, recede into your rituals, they exist to keep you safe. Mal's deepest rituals were nocturnal, unnoticeable even to himself.

Paris can be convinced. All they care about is the product. Delivery is what matters, everything else is negotiable.

He turns back to his man, who seems unnerved to be back within his eye-line. Mal isn't certain of his name: Brian? Colin, maybe? Ryan dealt with these things. The realisation causes a tremor in him. He smacks the bonnet of the MRAP. Takes one more moment for himself.

'Set up the billy-guns.'

Chapter 17

Even after the image cuts out, the screen still emits a silky black light. Ram craves darkness, some place to exist other than here, even just for a minute. He closes his eyes and tries to regulate his breath. His teeth are chattering, or maybe it's his jaws shivering or his whole skull - all he knows is that it's doing it on its own. Ram yearns for his mother: her voice, the smell of her room, the sheets. The thought of it makes him weep a little. The very tip of his tongue has been frosted and has finally fallen off. He spits its out, snaps open the visor and rockets it across the room. He's got to get a grip of this. He's got to keep it together.

Lazy is holding his brother, rocking and hushing him as if swaddling a baby. His fingers are two knuckles deep into the wounds, there's still warmth in there. Ram tries to talk to him but he snaps, almost foams with rage. Ram lets him blame him, throw Breen's blood at him, whatever he needs right now, Ram will give him. Eventually Lazy reverts to the hushing.

Now that the smoke has cleared, Ram can see the state of the place, walls burst apart, ceiling hanging, gore. The sound of flowing water draws his attention to the barricade, where the robot is slumped over the debris, right arm driven down into the floor, smiley face glaring at him creepily. Water is swirling and draining off somewhere.

Ram half-crawls over to investigate. Sure enough, the robot has punched a hole right through the floor and the water is spilling through. Ram reaches down, all the way to the elbow and then to the shoulder. The hollow slapping of water confirms it. There's a room down there, the basement.

He jolts upright, knowing what's next, though the idea's still only half-formed. He moves over to the cooker and begins whipping open the cupboard doors. He pulls out the canister of natural gas, a mustard-coloured tank with a collar. He carries it to where the water's swirling and wedges it between the robot's arm and where it's breached the floor. Needing something heavy to hold it in place, the best he can do is to bring the fridge down on top of it, partly pinning it. He clambers over to Lazy, and with his remaining hand grabs him by the face.

'Luca! Luca, listen to me. I'm not doing it, I'm not leaving my mom alone. You know, I've told you, he didn't even tell us he was sick. She never.... she never got to say goodbye to my dad. He just went out fucking wading and died. I can't do that to her again. I'm sorry for everything... I'm sorry for everything in the whole fucking world, but we are not done. I'm not done. Fuck. Them. They're just men, same as us. They're not taking any more. We're not letting them.'

Lazy stares blindly at him. 'I did it again,' he tells Ram. 'I left him in the woods again.'

'No, you didn't, you cunt. You didn't.'

'I'm his big brother.'

'Then act like it, Luca. You've got to stay angry. Please! You can't fall apart right now. They killed him, they killed Breen on us. Look, I'm going to do something and I need you to be ready. Are you ready?'

Lazy doesn't respond, he's somewhere else. Ram hugs him, brings him close. 'What did he want to do in Waterford? What did he want?'

Lazy pulls away, 'Dive. He wanted to dive.'

The beetle-bellied South African loading the mini-gun drops a belt of fifty calibre rounds and hunkers down for cover. The small explosion ricochets sound-waves across the yard.

'What was that?' someone shouts.

Mal stares at the house, his face beginning to betray him. He looks worried, too many pieces moving at once. A puff of dust rolls from the front door and dies in the headlight lit rain. He's going to kill that dog if it doesn't stop barking.

'Get it fucking done, lads!' he shouts back.

The South African signals that he's ready. Brian-Colin signals from his truck that he's ready too. They call the guns 'billy goats', because they'll eat anything, their barrels are spinning, whizzing, hungry. Mal kicks the MRAP door closed. He's not going to shoot the dog yet.

He points at the house and calls out, 'Eat!'

The industrial grind of automated fire explodes across the yard, its concussive bass loud enough to penetrate chest cavities and myocardial rhythms. Two broken lines of light appear as if they've existed all along, only now becoming visible through lenses of extreme velocity and copper-jacketed lead. The farmhouse absorbs the fire, walls popping, bursting apart. An engine revs and the truck carrying the South African strafes across the yard, its stream of bullets shearing an antler from the head of the statue on its course.

His hip makes a hot, hollow pop as he comes up into the dark. It hurts to breathe. One of the short ribs on his right side is broken or badly bruised. His prosthetic is aggravating the injury, so he removes it and leaves it behind. Above him, the gunfire sounds like a combine harvester chewing through the house.

'Lazy, you there?' he asks the air. Even talking hurts.

A red-hot light burns incandescently just ahead of him before degenerating into a hissing, glowing sphere. He raises his stump instinctively to shield his eyes. It's a flare. It smells just like your fingers right after you've quenched a match between them.

'Just about.'

Aided by the light from the flare, they attempt to get a feel for the size of the basement. The flickering, spastic light reveals the breath of the massive space.

'This isn't a basement, it's like, a bunker or warehouse or something,' Ram tells him. 'Old RA stash-house maybe?'

Lazy, buckling under his own weight, reaches out searching for something steady to hold onto. His fingers find the cool skeletal frame of warehouse shelving.

The pain is becoming coherent again, the knot around his leg wound loosening. He stares up at the ceiling, where the tumbling water is wrinkling what little light is making it through the gash in the ceiling.

'I don't know about that, never heard of one this big. Man, that's a twenty-five-foot drop.'

'You got another one of those?' Ram asks, pointing to the flare.

'Two.'

Ram crouches in front of him, assessing the wound as best he can in the light. He grabs the comb, Lazy winces.

'You gotta keep this tight,' Ram tells him.

'I'm fine. Let's look around.'

The munching above them stops for a moment, and when it returns it has changed in volume and pitch.

'They're firing lower, trying to make sure…'

'This place is so big we could walk right under them.'

'Let's just concentrate on the walking part for now.'

They start to move through the bunker, lumbering along arm in arm. To their right, rows of warehouse shelving, stacked with everything from racks of ammunition to cans of beans and soup. There are wooden pallets filled with boxes and vacuum-packed blankets, bags of sand, cement, porridge oats. Lazy stubs his foot on a red plastic food cooler. He leans over and knocks off the lid with his rifle, inside he finds thick cuts of yellowed bacon doused in sea salt.

'You know, I'm starving and I still wouldn't eat that shit.'

Lazy rests on the edge of a shelf. 'Fuck, hold on. I need a minute.'

'Fine. Give me one of those flares and stay here. We don't have much time. I'm going to take a look around.'

Ram enters into the dimness where the dark widens and reveals something shimmering in the centre of the room. He pulls the cap off the flare with his teeth and smacks the bottom off the bonnet of the vehicle, then suddenly sees himself appear in the windscreen of a small yellow pick-up truck, barely taller than he is.

'What you got over there?' asks Lazy from across the room.

Rooting through the cab of the truck, Ram shouts back,' Nothing much, just an old truck. Old-old.'

Lazy drags his leg behind him, dead below the knee, ravenous above it, the wound feels like a rat is trying to tunnel through his knee, every step another nervy nibble. He's only moved a few feet before something catches his attention, a vaguely rectangular box standing upright against the wall, glinting at him, right next to the shelves where he had been resting. He slumps towards it, intrigued by its eerie amber aura. This dim rippling light seems to be emanating from the bottom of the box, as he draws closer it reveals itself to be not a rectangle but a cylinder.

His flare is barely an ember now, so he tosses it and lights the last one. As it burns he assumes for a second that it's his own reflection he sees in the glass, but it is not. He freezes, stunned, gawking up through the glass. It's a water tank, and floating inside it is, unmistakably, a person. Two arms, two legs, genitalia, the tight, sinewy frame of a man, bollock-naked apart for his hands which are both gloved and bound.

He draws closer, straining to get a look at the man's face, but it's hidden within some kind of thick woolly filament that enshrouds his skull all the way down past the throat. The way this shroud moves in the water is almost plant-like, resembling some species of ocean cotton you find amid fields of deep-sea coral. The only movement inside is the dreamy sway of the filaments, and the micro-bubbles waltzing up from the bottom of the tank. He lays his hands against the glass, which is tepid to the touch and thick enough to barely ring when he knocks on it.

He whips around to shout out to Ram, but is struck by the flash of florescent lights burning. The ceiling lights are only up for a second before they short out, sending sparks and electrical feedback raining through the bunker. Lazy's back in the dark again, dead skins of light snaking around his vision. He hears the clapping of electrical junction boxes and then Ram's voice, energetic, manic.

'Holy mother of fuck! Lazy! Luca, come over here.'

Just getting as far as the truck is agony, his wound is muddy and every step sends complex circuits of pain lancing up through him. He's dizzy and his lips are cracked so dry that they bleed. His brother comes to him in waves, the thought of him, still up there in the house alone. Pain crowds him, fiddles with his connections. He has to rest. He leans against the truck for a moment. Ram still calling for him.

Leaning against the corner of the cab, he rests his head against the cool glass of the window and turns toward Ram's light. Ram is just ahead, a one-armed silhouette holding a fading star, he's opposite something hulking and padded with bulky armour. There's glass, painted steel and huge closed fists, knuckles wresting guerrilla-like against the bunker floor. Water has run across the roof and is dripping everywhere.

Lazy burrows through his internal filing cabinet, searching for some reference to what he's looking at. He's fading a little, eyes almost closed. Suddenly a different circuit lights up in him, an overwhelming muddle of shock and cautious excitement.

'Jesus, Mary and Joseph, is that what I think it is? Can you drive it? Are there keys?' he asks, wide-eyed.

Ram turns, his eyes black holes in the reddening flare-light. 'You've never looked these up?'

'I've better things to do with my time.'

'Yeah, well, you're not "generation carbon fibre", are you?'

'Just tell me you got keys.'

Ram tosses the flare, regards the guerrilla-knuckles and then begins to climb them. He straddles the sides of the entrance, the scooped-out innards of the machine, and drops down into the cockpit. Sitting back against the pilot's seat, stiff leather pinching his bare lower back, he takes a calming breath, his lower jaw quivering with adrenaline.

The *proprioceptor* slides into the hole below his collarbone and he experiences that familiar feeling in his forehead, like a rush of bubbles. A beeping noise precedes an array of holographic lights streaming down his face, scrolling like end-credits. A female voice welcomes him to *Rednitz Military Solutions* while several layers of glass and metal begin to close around him, enveloping him in the chest of the Covjec. As the steel and bullet-proof glass begins to swallow him, elegant as tulip petals, he smiles through the remaining gap.

'You've got to get with the program, Jack. I am the keys.'

A fist-sized sphere bounces against a wall, splashing down beside the staircase. It bobs noiselessly in the water before hushing out a stiff spray of some chemical aerosol. It begins to blink with red light, illuminating the body at the foot of the stairs. The blinking stops, and a moment later the downstairs hallway is a mass of blue flame.

Outside, Mal watches through the doorway as the flames take the house, stepping back as a proud plume of acerbic smoke rises. A man ambles into his peripheral, a jaundice-faced fellow by the name of Bill Prendergast.

'Will downstairs be all right?' he asks.

Mal looks at him side-eyed, 'It survived the end of the world.'

Chapter 18

Warning: Unable to access Hoplite satellite network, certain network features will remain unavailable. Warning: you are running an illegally modified edition of Middle/dutch-8OS. Primary account locked. Please contact Bryce Rednitz Bloom support services to unlock this rig's primary account. Would you like to create a guest account?

'Yes, I would.'

Controller settings: I am detecting a neurohaptic port. Would you like to open a signalling plane to Hoplite motor systems?

'Yes.'

Temporary user name required.

'Stumpy.'

Password required.

'vikingfuneral.'

Guest1 account created. Pinging neurohaptic gateway. Bearer found, context 'Brazen-Head'. Hoplite Motor systems online. Manual control handover complete. Caution: Hoplite crew is live. Visok-čovječ hardware is live. My name is IRMA. How may I help you, operator?

Mal takes a snort of snuff straight from the box, it burns a fuse up into his sinuses.

'Take someone and go sweep around the house,' he tells Prendergast. 'We don't leave till we see bodies. And I want to know what happened to Ronan and Ryan - '

He is suddenly cut off by a pneumatic quaking beneath him,

strong enough to make his heels tingle. His heart thumps at the back of his face.

'What was that?' Prendergast asks, face blank.

Mal knows exactly what it is.

'Weapons hot at the lift!'

The warped aching of gears becomes audible in the garden. Two sheets of steel rise from the centre of the slurry-pit, reaching seven foot or more. They yawn outwards, shoving water and wooden planks clear of the lift's trajectory. In response to Mal's orders, the men organise themselves into a loose crescent, weapons checked, safeties off. The billy-gun operators swivel and spin their barrels, ready to fire. Mal waits at the back, checking his pockets for the handgun.

As the lift slowly rises water drops, sending a cool spray through the men.

'How the fuck did they get down there?' Brian-Colin shouts from his turret.

'They may not have,' Mal replies. 'It could be an emergency thing… from an alarm, or something.'

Jittering with adrenaline, the men watch as the lift rises to meet the roof of the open-faced barn, its frame shivering to a stop, clanging with chains and cables. The scene becomes still, dioramic, there's no sound except the ping-pong of rain on aluminium. The closest man to the barn takes a cautious initiative, he peers around the edges of the ramp, his weapon raised, shouldered tightly. He reaches in, slaps a red button and drops his arms in relief as the ramp descends slowly. An uneasy calm whispers through the group as they regard the lift, waiting for the magician's curtain to finally drop. It lowers enough to allow them to see inside, and there it is: just that old yellow truck.

Bill Prendergast looks at Mal with a nervous half-smile. He blows out a breath through slitted lips and wipes the rain off his face in a single wide stroke.

'Jesus, Mary and Joseph! For a second there, lads, I thought it was going to be the- '

From his vantage on the truck's turret, the South African watches the huge swell of water explode around Prendergast. A great guerrilla hand spears out from the depths and snatches him. There is a mythological quality to it, Norse, Greek, the hand of an ice giant reaching out from Jötunheimr. The hand has an arm and a shoulder, and then it is climbing out of the underworld in a torrent of sound and motion. He hears the giant before he can see it clearly, the glassy mist chirping with the exhaust sounds of hydraulics and heavy steel hitting earth. There are enormous movements and the shine of vinyl. And then the shadow of it looms, fifteen or twenty feet high. He knows what it is but it shouldn't be possible. Only Ryan can drive her.

Spotlights spring into life from its shoulders, blinding the already disorientated men. The South African shields his eyes. He can just about make out the red print on the giant's shoulder, it's Croatian: *Visok-čovječ*, it means 'tall man'. He knows this because at the time he asked. Translated for him by Ryan in a field in Llanwym, Wales, where they drank Rakia from the lid of a flask and raised a toast to a job well done, vessels raised to the stolen Tall-Man, a tank folded around the frame of a man, its guts splayed open among the bog cotton and moor grass, operated on by experts, hacked before the owners had even noticed it missing. East European hardware, German-American software.

Time is stewing, his gun barrel is spinning but if he fires, fuck knows what he'll hit. The Covjec stands in the garden, framed by the burning house. Its bipedal legs, bird-like in its pelvic girdle, adjusting to the cracked ground and floodwater in fluid, complex movements. The South African stares at the Covjec's right hand, Prendergast's legs dangling like keys between its fingers. A man panics, fires and is swatted like the head of a reed, flying so fast it's impossible to know which part of him has gone where. Malik rises from the water, the back of his head warm and throbbing. He calls for fire and the men oblige, both turrets screaming histrionically towards their target.

Operating the Covjec feels familiar, like using his prosthetic or navigating the drone, only those were VHS and this is Neurosynaptic High Definition Video. The haptic responses are so clear and crisp that they become indistinguishable from his own muscles, at times it feels as if the machine is driving him, using him as a resource, a mobile endocrine system. His eyes are cameras mounted behind bulletproof plastics. Men wear red haloes. He's searching for one halo in particular when the bullets find him.

Warning: Receiving Incoming fire. Targets identified. Weapon systems online. Ammunition count: 0 rounds loaded. Lapwing missile count: 0 rounds loaded.

'You could have mentioned that earlier, Irma.'

Two streams of bullets meet on the chest of the Tall-Man, sending out a waterfall of sparks. The South African drops his aim to the legs, where the Covjec looks most vulnerable. Brian-Colin concentrates on the arms, almost deaf from the roaring guns. Ram grabs the only thing he can, the statue. The Covjec wrenches the statue out of the ground in one whole piece and throws it at Brian-Colin's truck. The impact sends the truck tumbling through a stable, where it explodes.

Lazy sits up from his position at the bottom of the truck's CAB and regards the scene through the windscreen. He can't feel his leg anymore, and while he was down against the old leather seat cover he's sure he blacked out for a moment, but this is all fine. He opens the door and leans outside, positioning his machine gun between the door-frame and the cab. He sees the Tall-Man rip the statue from the yard and throw it at one of the trucks. He sees a man, a weak one, turn and start to run. He fires in short, controlled bursts and then calmly moves on to the next.

Operator: Ammunition counts are available on the bottom right-hand corner of your heads-up display.

'That's good to know, but not much use to me. What weapons have I got?'

Flame-thrower fuel cells are at 46%. Puddle Jumper grapple line is loaded.

Ram aims an arm at the South African and hears a rush of liquid from beneath him. The South African releases his trigger and tries to leap from the cab, but the ignition is already lit. The truck is engulfed in red flame. The South African flails to the ground, yelling for help that isn't coming. A burning man is an easy target, Lazy fires, hitting head and throat. The trucks windscreen shatters, he's been noticed this time. The door frame kicks and he feels a hot poker pass through him. He wrestles himself into the cab for cover, firing blindly over the dashboard.

Mal grabs a man by the back of the neck and orders him into the remaining truck, barking at him, 'Use the fucking rocket-launcher!'

A man approaches the barn, cocksure that he's tagged the person hiding in the truck. Lazy is still firing blindly, hitting nothing but air. The guy sees a head in the gap between the door and the truck, he aims, and is about to fire when the rain suddenly becomes tepid and rank with petrol. He goes up in a fireball, another easy target.

Ram spots the red halo he's been searching for, Malik, shouting orders at the handful of men left alive and able-bodied. He strides toward him, his intentions set on crushing him underfoot, then a whoooosh! strikes the Covjec in the right hip. The explosion sends the Tall-Man's legs flying back from under it. Ram rattles inside the cockpit, his nose bloodied from butting something in the display. Anti-heat-seeking flares fire uselessly from the back of the suit, and the Tall-Man lands on its hands and knees, alarms blaring. Ram is scared for a moment. This loss of concentration makes it harder for him to operate the suit, the arms aren't responding fast enough and the hips begin to rotate back and forth.

Mal orders the man to reload the launcher. The man does as he's told, sliding a missile down into the smoking tube. He shoulders the launcher, his hands sore and slippery. The robot is up on one knee, almost upright.

Puddle Jumper Line unlocked. Please designate target.

The grapple hits the man so hard and so fast that he barely feels it. He is simply sheared into quadrants, nothing left but a quick bright mist and a single standing leg. His head and shoulders are still in the palm of the grapple, which has carried on through him and into the truck behind. The truck folds in on itself and flips on its side. The rocket launches at the sky, exploding beautifully in low cloud. In the flash the Tall-Man comes up, a wheeze of steam misting from its back.

A trickle of blood runs down Ram's face, splitting into vectors below his nostrils. Suddenly a sheet of flame explodes across the body of the suit, and then another. A man is lobbing incendiary grenades from somewhere, following orders, creating a distraction. Mal is making his way to the South African's truck, the only one that still has wheels on the ground, the flames dampened.

Ram catches a glimpse of a red halo in the stables. He makes for the building, upper-cutting thought the walls and roof. He drives a foot down into the building and twists. Suddenly he's being hit by machine-gun fire, catching him off balance. He drops into the stables, lashed by bullets from the billy-gun. Ram tries to rise, pieces of armour spinning off the hull. The end-credits on his face turn amber and then red, Irma warns of a breach. He can smell smoke. Arm held aloft as if he's protecting himself from a school bully, he stands up. The display is chaos, the force of the impacts vibrating through his chest and teeth. He rushes the truck, swaying in the gunfire.

Mal knows it's not going to be enough. He waits until he has to and then jumps clear. Ram punches down through the vehicle and it folds up, exploding around him. The truck lifts into the air and Ram pulls it apart, striding through the flames. Mal watches him approach, rising to greet him, Ram's father's gun held aloft. The Tall-Man looms above him in silent regard, flames still spitting in the rain. Ram wants to see him with his own two eyes, wants to hear that smoke cured voice. He opens the first layer of the cockpit.

The chest of the Tall-Man unfolds, revealing the driver inside. Mal fires a shot that ricochets off the bullet-proof glass. He fires again with the same result. Two more shots leave nothing but a scuff on the windscreen. Ram regards him through the glass, watching the firelight tug at the shallows of his face. The image has a dreamy quality. A magic mirror quality. The water and the man and the fire and the slow-motion weather. *What do you do with a man like this?* The next bullet sends a crack bifurcating into the glass, right through the profile of Ram's face.

Mal shouts defiantly, 'Come on out, you fucking townie piece of shit. I'm more scared of me mother, and she's dead and fucking buried. I'll scalp you, you prick!'

He fires again, his aim surgical. Ram flinches in the pilot seat. Chips spin out from the impact. Mal whoops, arms manic. He fires once more, but this time the gun clicks impotently. The clip is empty, it sounds like a stapler. It's not a weapon anymore, it's office equipment. Ram expects him to run but he doesn't. Mal's eyes are still fuzzy black holes, but by the way his face is tilted to the sky Ram knows they're closed. He's enjoying the cool strokes of the rain on his face. His chest rises in a slow, deep breath. He soothes the air.

'Got anything for himself?' Mal asks, calm, addressing the sky. *What do you do with a man like this?*

A closed fist, the weight of a forklift, pounds Mal into the ground. Bubbles burp to the surface of light-dazzled water, black orbs in the white. The inner chest of the Tall-Man opens and Ram spills out, cables and harnesses still attached.

He lands on elbow and knees, the imagery is not lost on him. Unhinging himself from the machine, he trawls beneath the surface for the pistol. When he finds it, he has to prise it from Mal's severed hand.

He places the gun behind the belt of his trousers, it is cold and oily against his stomach. As he comes up, some fluid runs down the inside of his thigh, there is a bizarre relief in its warm snaking between the hairs. He turns around, puzzled, wondering why the hell he's hearing barking from the flipped-over truck. It's the one he'd hit with the grapple, the line still sagging over the side, right between the legs of a man, one ankle is still twitching.

An image of Luca comes to him.

He makes his way to the barn, navigating cautiously through the scrum of bodies and flaming wrecks, half expecting a vengeful bullet or two to come searching for him.

The smell of the burning house and the smoke from its bones yawn across the yard, heating him, scratching the inside of his nostrils. The engine of the yellow truck turns over in the barn, its headlights dim and spectral. Lazy is in the driver's seat, twiddling his beard, waxy little wicks flat with blood. Hearing the sound of his breathing, Ram starts to cry. It's not the pucks in Lazy's chest or the blinking gape in his throat that start him off, it's the sound of his best friend on the planet drowning on dry land.

Lazy moves his eyes in a way that suggests he thinks he's turning to face Ram, but he isn't.

'I didn't leave him.'

'No, you didn't, brother. You did not.'

Watching Luca die is not pleasant. The naked plea in his eyes, the way they bulge now, it invades Ram, dissembles him spiritually. He feels overwhelmingly ashamed. Ashamed to be the one here at this moment, to see this. It's like an awful, unwanted gift he's being forced to open. A father should be here for this, or a mother, or a brother. He strokes Luca's hair, dabbing beneath his eyes. Eyes that, as panic sets in, begin to recede into their infancy. Ten minutes earlier if his own life depended on it, Ram couldn't have told you what colour those eyes were. *Caffe crema*, rough, kind.

The air currents carry half-whispers, bits of prayers, perhaps his mother's name. A clot the size of a crab-apple drops from a wound. As Luca passes, his lips begin to move, mouthing something that Ram can't make out. He kisses him on the cheeks and forehead, checks his chest for life, and rests his hands on the steering wheel one last time.

Chapter 19

The aul' fella sits in his golf cart, a slip of a man, sharp shoulders, fishing rod posture. His suit jacket is an over-worn tweed, speckle grey. Musk is a primary attribute. It's bearable out in the open, but indoors, it's a hostage crisis.

Legs crossed, cramped into the steering wheel, he reads his paperback, folded to fit in one hand, his other hand groping the bowl of his pipe. His cat snoozes above him, splayed across the grotty roof, its fur seasoned with catkins from the alder canopy.

Slieve na Much sounds leaky this morning, but it's warm and humid and the radio is humming. There's been a noise in the sky for minutes, it's getting louder. He peers out from under the cart for a nose. Helicopters.

The cat perceives something stir beneath the sensory horizon, opening its eyes reluctantly. Vibrations ripple through the white vinyl. There's a thumping now, a weighty clunk on the tarmac.

Two younger men emerge from their cabin. They stand at the barrier, a repurposed old-world railway crossing, and look down the hill. The aul' fella rattles the ignition and drives to meet them, the cart buzzing, the cat spinning and landing safely on four paws.

Sunlight over-exposes the image, catching sleek oxidised steel. The Hoplite rides the crest of the hill, lumbering towards them. The men regard each other, adjust their waistbands, fidget with anticipation, take selfies.

The Hoplite is wounded, parts exposed, skin sheared along

the limbs and chest. It's dragging something heavy with it up the hill, lifted up on its back wheels: the *Lion of St. Mark*.

Stopping at the barrier, the *St. Mark* drops, bobbing on its suspension. The choking of gears precedes a genuflection, drawing its chest closer to the ground. The men move a step back, take more pictures.

A sinkful of water leaks from the opening chassis, the tulip leaves of the cockpit's armour, then the internal glass shell beneath, with its ominous cracks. A Yorkshire terrier lands on the gravel, panting happily at the men as she yoga-poses into a peeing posture. Ram doesn't even try to miss the puddle, flopping out of the cockpit onto all fours.

The aul' fella leans over the steering-wheel.

'Jesus, Mary and Joseph - where's his arm?'

'That's Ram Gallagher's young fella. I think it's always been like that,' one of them explains.

'Are you all right, Ray?' asks the other, handing Ram a half-drunk bottle of juice.

Ram swallows it appreciatively while the terrier takes off after the cat. The helicopters are hovering above him. He reaches for a hand up, the man obliges but Ram struggles.

'Can you take me home, please?' he asks.

'Barry, will you get off her and let us drive him up town?'

'Can we do a swap?' jokes the aul' fella with a gunky, happy laugh.

Arm bent around the back of his new friend's neck, Ram nods, exhausted. 'She's all yours.'

The two men load Ram into the golf cart, emptying out the crisp packets and three-dimensional plastic triangles, sandwich boxes, all smeared with the same stinky tikka. Before they take off, Ram notices the aul' fella poking around the *St. Mark*.

'Something banging back there. Have you an animal under that tarp?'

Ram replies, 'I'm not sure what it is, Barry... Best leave it to our friends up there.'

The terrier reappears and leaps up on him, declawed paws scrambling at his bare chest. They drive him uphill, cold air pimpling his skin.

They exit the shade of the canopy and the sun meets them, its heat speaking to him in beating strokes. He's driving through a memory, the morning after his Grads' party.

Strolling up the hill towards town, humming of the night, suit jacket lost, buzzed from the two yokes and the shift on the bus home. All he wanted was sleep, and when he got home he crept into his parents' bed and slept soundly in the smell of their sheets. His dad woke him at dinner time with tea and lemon curd toast. He was going to do that again. He was going to sleep in that bed whenever he got to sleep again, after he'd spoken to whoever the hell he was going to have to speak to, however many times.

He fingers the dog's collar and unhinges the clasp: pink with a diamanté rim. Her name is spelled out in white gold: *Colette.* He throws it into the glen, he has one for her at home.

He closes his eyes and thinks about that morning once more, the smell of those sheets.

The End

Acknowledgments

I would like to say thank you to Maverick House for allowing me to bring this story to people. For believing Ireland is a place where stories like this can exist. To my parents for raising me so close to such a beautiful place like Aherlow in Tipperary. To Dad for forcing me to learn Boolavogue all those years ago. To Lindsey for her patience. To Dave Higgins for his always honest feedback and encouragement. To Keith and Neil for their advice on Drones.

To Piercarlo for his help with authentic Italian translation.

And to Eileen for her help with the early draft.